Six Nights Of Sins
The Complete Series

Books 1-6

(A La Petite Mort Club Series)

Ellis O. Day

I love to hear from readers so email me at
authorellisoday@gmail.com

Facebook
https://www.facebook.com/EllisODayRomanceAuthor/

Twitter
https://twitter.com/ellis_o_day

Pinterest
www.pinterest.com\AuthorEllisODay

Other Books By Ellis O. Day:

THE VOYEUR SERIES EBOOK
The Voyeur (Book One) **FREE**
Watching the Voyeur (Book Two)
Touching the Voyeur (Book Three)
Loving the Voyeur (Book Four)

The Voyeur Series (all four books)
(ebook and paperback)

Six Weeks of Seduction
(Nick and Sarah's HEA)

A Merry Masquerade For Christmas

Book 1

Interviewing For Her Lover

CHAPTER 1: SARAH

"Do I have to take off my clothes?" Sarah tugged on the hem of her black dress. It was shorter and lower cut in the front than she normally wore, but the Viewing was about finding a man for sex and according to Ethan men liked to look.

"No." Ethan turned her away from the door and forced her to look at him. "You don't have to do anything you don't want to do."

She stared into his blue eyes. Why couldn't he be interested in her? She'd only met with him five or six times, but she trusted him. He ran his business, La Petite Mort Club, very professionally and he was gorgeous with his sandy brown hair, strong cheekbones and vibrant blue eyes. Sex between them would be good. Easy. He was attractive and…not for her. She didn't want decent sex or good sex, she wanted mind blowing, screaming orgasms and that wouldn't happen between him and her because there was no chemistry, no attraction.

"Listen to me." He moved his hands to her shoulders and gave her a gentle shake. "You aren't selling yourself to the highest bidder. You're looking for a partner. One who'll"—he grinned—"turn you on in ways you can't even imagine."

She glanced at the door where the men waited. Waited for her. Waited to decide if they wanted to fuck her. "I'm a bit nervous."

"About what?"

This was embarrassing but she'd been honest with him up to this point. She'd had to be. He was helping her...had helped her to choose the five men in the other room. "What if none of them..."

"They will want you." He touched her chin, turning her face toward him. "A few of them may back out after this but not because they don't want you."

"Yeah, right."

"I'm only going to say this once. You're beautiful and different, unique."

"That's not necessarily a good thing." She had long legs and a nice body—trim and firm—but with her auburn hair and green eyes she was cute at best, not gorgeous. The men she'd chosen were all rich, good looking and powerful. They could have anyone they wanted.

"It's exactly what they want, or most of them anyway." He took her hand and led her closer to the door.

She leaned on his arm, hating these shoes. She should've stuck with her flats but Ethan had given her a list of what she should wear and high heels were on the top. She'd found the smallest heels in the store and by Ethan's look when he'd first seen her she might've been better off going barefoot. He'd met her at the private entrance and his gaze had been appreciating as it'd skimmed over her dress, until he got to her feet. Then he'd frowned and shook his head.

"Finding the right men for you wasn't easy." He stopped at the door.

"Thanks a lot." She shifted away from him, his words hurting a little. She hadn't been sure of her appeal to the opposite sex in a long time, not since the early years with Adam.

"It's not because you aren't beautiful but because you want to be dominated and you want to dominate—"

"I do not want to dominate." All she could picture was a woman in black leather with a whip and that wasn't her, not at all.

"If you say so." He smiled a little. "But, you do want to lead the scene. Right? Because that's what—"

"Yes." Her face was red. She could feel it. She didn't want to talk about her fantasies again. It'd been embarrassing enough the first time, but he'd had to know what she wanted to compile a list of candidates.

"Most at the club are either doms or subs. Very few are switches." His eyes raked over her. "That's what's so special about you. You want it all and…that's what made choosing these men difficult."

He'd given her a selection of twenty-two men who might be interested in what she wanted. She'd narrowed it down to seven. Two had been uninterested when he'd approached. That'd left her with the five who'd see her in person for the first time tonight, but she wouldn't see them.

That'd come after the Viewing when she interviewed any who were still interested.

"Remember what you want. This is your deal. You call the shots. At least a little." He kissed her forehead. "But don't refuse to give them anything. You don't want a submissive."

"No." That didn't turn her on at all and she only had eight weeks. One night each week for two months before she'd go back to her lonely life, her lonely bed, dreaming of Adam.

"You can do this." He pulled a flask from his jacket and unscrewed the lid. "For courage."

"Thanks." She took a large swallow, the brandy too thick and sweet for her taste but it was better than nothing.

"Now, go find your lover."

She laughed a little but sadness swept through her. There'd be no love between this man and herself. This would be sex, fucking. That's all. The only man she'd ever love, her only lover, was dead. This was purely physical. "Thank you again." She stood on tip-toe and kissed his cheek. He may be gorgeous and run a sex club but he was a good man, a good friend.

She turned and opened the door and walked into the room, trying to stay balanced on these stupid heels. Men wouldn't find them so attractive if they had to wear them. The room was dark except for one light highlighting a small platform. That was for her. She stepped up onto the small stage. The room was silent but they were there, above her, hidden behind the one-way mirrors, watching and deciding if they wanted to take the next step—to eventually take her.

4

She stared into the blackness of the room. It wasn't huge but its emptiness made it seem vast. She glanced upward, the light making her squint and she quickly stared back into the darkness. This was arranged for them to see her. That was it. She'd get no glimpse of them yet. She'd seen their pictures, chosen them but meeting them in person would be different. A picture couldn't tell her their smell or the sound of their voices.

She tugged at her dress where it hugged her hips, wishing the questions would start, but there was only silence. She shifted, the heels already killing her feet. Ethan hadn't liked them and if they weren't going to impress, she might as well take them off. She moved to the back of the stage, leaned against the wall and removed her shoes. As she returned to the center of the stage a man spoke, his voice loud and commanding almost echoing throughout the room.

"Don't stop there. Take off your dress."

She bent, placing her shoes on the floor. That wasn't part of the deal. She wasn't going to undress in front of five men, only one. Only the one she chose. She straightened. "No."

"What?" He was surprised and not happy.

"I said no. That's not part of the Viewing."

"I want to see what I'm getting."

She stared up toward the windows, squinting a little. She couldn't tell from where the voice had come. The speaker system made it sound as if it were coming from God himself. "And you will if I pick you."

Another man laughed.

"It's not funny. She's disobedient," said the man

with the loud voice.

"Not always. I can be obedient." These men liked to be in control but sometimes, so did she.

"Will you raise your dress? Just a little," asked another voice.

"Didn't you see enough in the photos?" She'd applied a few months ago for this one-time contract. She'd been excited and nervous when she'd received the acceptance email with an appointment for a photography session. She'd never had her picture professionally taken, since she didn't count school portraits or the ones her parents had had done at JCPenny's. She'd been anxious and a little turned on imaging wearing her new lingerie in front of a strange man, so she'd been disappointed to find the photographer was an elderly woman, but the lady had put her at ease and the photos had turned out better than she'd expected. She glanced up at the mirrors, hoping she wasn't disappointing all the men. That'd be too embarrassing.

"Those were…nice, but I'd like to see the real thing before deciding if you're worth my time."

She raised a brow. "You can always leave." She shouldn't antagonize him. She was sure the bossy man had already decided against committing to this agreement. Disobedience didn't appeal to him. That left four. If she didn't pick any of them, she could go through the process again, but she didn't think she would.

The man chuckled slightly. "I know that, but I haven't decided I don't want to fuck you. Not yet, anyway."

The word, so harsh and vulgar excited her. It was

the truth. That was what she, what they were all deciding. Who'd get to fuck her. It was what she wanted, what she'd agreed to do, and as much as she dreaded it, she wanted it. She was tired of being alone. She missed having a man inside her—his tongue and fingers and cock.

"Do any of you have any questions?" She clasped her dress at her waist and slowly gathered it upward, displaying more and more of her long legs. She ran. They were in shape. The men would like them.

"Lower your top," said the same man who'd told her to take off her dress.

She didn't like him. If he didn't back out, she'd have Ethan remove him from her list. He was too commanding. He'd never allow her to be in control.

"I don't know if he's done looking at my legs yet." She continued raising the dress until her black and green lace panties were almost exposed.

"Very nice and thank you," said the polite man.

"You're welcome." This man might work. She shifted the dress up another inch before dropping it, giving them a glance at her panties.

"Now, your top," said the bossy guy.

She lowered her spaghetti string off one shoulder, letting the dress dip, but not enough to show anything besides the side of her bra.

"More," he said.

"No." She raised the strap, covering herself. She didn't like this man and wished he'd leave. She'd kick him out but that wasn't part of the process and they were very firm about their rules at this club.

"He got to see your pussy. Why don't I get to see

your tits?"

"You got to see as much as he did." She was ready to move on. She bent and picked up her shoes. "If there's nothing else, gentleman, we can set up times for the interview process."

"Turn around," said another man.

It was a command, but she didn't mind. There was a politeness to his order and something about the texture of his voice caused an ache between her thighs. There was a caress in his tone but with an edge and a promise of a good hard fuck.

"Are you going to obey?" His words were whisper soft and smooth.

"Yes." That was going to be part of this too. Her commanding and him commanding. She dropped her shoes and turned.

"Raise you dress again."

She looked over her shoulder at where she imagined he sat watching her.

"Please." There was humor in his tone.

She smiled and slowly gathered the dress upward. She stopped right below the curve of her bottom.

"More. Please." There was a little less humor in his voice.

She wanted to show him her ass. She wanted to show that voice everything but not with the others around. This would be just her and one man, one stranger. That was one of her rules. "No. Only if you're picked do you get to see any more of me than you have." She dropped her dress, grabbed her shoes and walked off the stage and out the door.

She was going to have sex with a stranger. She was going to live out her fantasies for eight nights with a man she didn't know and would never really know, but she wasn't going to lose who she was. She'd keep her honor and her dignity which meant she had to pick a man who'd agree with her rules.

CHAPTER 2: NICK

Nick wanted her. A lot. His dick pushed against the zipper of his pants and he plucked at the cloth, trying to make himself more comfortable. He hadn't wanted to fuck anyone this badly in a very long time. He wasn't sure exactly what it was about her that made him want to dominate her. She was cute, sexy even but he'd had hotter women. His eyes caressed her stiff, straight back as she began to raise her dress for Patrick. Something about the way she'd refused to obey when Terry had ordered her to undress had made him want to bend her to his rule. To mold her to his desires until they were hers too. Terry, the idiot, would break her, change her into a submissive.

She had nice legs, long and smooth. He grinned as she flashed them a quick look at her panties before dropping her dress. Black lace was typical, but he was almost certain there was green lace interwoven in them too. Green like her eyes. He had to find out.

She lowered the strap of her dress and he sucked in

a breath as his hand adjusted himself again. This was getting painful, but he couldn't take his eyes from her. With her long auburn hair, pale skin and green eyes she looked like an Irish fairy from his grandmother's tales. Beautiful, magical and dangerous.

Terry bellowed at her again. She'd leave if that kept up and he'd never see her panties. That wouldn't do. Not at all. "Turn around." He said it as an order but with a hint of a plea.

After some discussion, she obeyed.

"Raise your dress again." He really needed to see her panties. "Please."

She lifted her dress almost displaying her ass. His hand stroked across his cock. Oh yeah, he'd fuck that. She hadn't raised it high enough for him to see if there were green in her panties, but it no longer mattered.

Patrick's polite thank you as she walked out the door made him pause. He should let Patrick have her. Patrick was a good guy and would treat her right, do exactly what she wanted. He shifted in his seat, his erection painfully hard in its confinement. He should let Patrick have her, but he wouldn't. He pressed the button on the chair and the door opened.

Veronica strolled in, all lush curves and softness. She was one of his favorites, always up for anything.

"Nicky, baby you're all worked up." Veronica's brown eyes stared at the bulge in his pants and slowly raised to his face. As soon as his eyes met hers, she licked her lush, red lips.

"Knees." He wasn't in the mood to play.

She strolled forward, her hips rolling seductively.

He usually enjoyed watching her work, but tonight he didn't want a lush, full-figured platinum blonde. He wanted an auburn-haired fairy. He spread his legs, giving her better access and leaned back his head, closing his eyes.

It was Sarah not Veronica, kneeling before him. She wore only dark green panties—her breasts bare and her lips full and pink. It was her tongue that darted out, licking his tip, tasting him. Her hand stroked his length while her mouth and tongue worked the tip of his cock, sucking and licking. She felt so good, so hot and wet and…the suction was intense. His balls tightened and his dick got even bigger, but Sarah kept sucking. He came hard and fast, spurting in her mouth. He imagined Sarah swallowing every bit and licking her lips. His dick twitched and started to harden but he didn't have time to come again. He opened his eyes. Veronica gave him one last lick, to clean him off and then dabbed at her lips, her red lipstick still dark and intact. He put his semi-flaccid dick back in his pants and zipped them up.

"Thank you, Veronica." He reached for his wallet and handed her a couple of hundreds. The service was free, part of the membership to the club, but good tips kept the best girls coming.

"Should I stay?" Her hand trailed up his thigh.

It wouldn't be too long before he could go again and Veronica was fun, but she wasn't who he wanted. "Not tonight."

She frowned a little as she stood. "If you change your mind, I'm here until midnight." She waved at him as she left.

He poured himself another drink. It was tempting,

but he didn't have time for a night of sex. His interview could be tomorrow or the next day and he had to win. He had to have Sarah and that meant he had to beat his competition.

Terry was out, but the others weren't going to lose without a fight. Ethan wouldn't help him. His friend took the rules of his club seriously. No, he had to decipher what she wanted by himself. He opened her dossier, paying closer attention to her desires and fantasies than he'd done before. It wasn't going to be easy to figure out what she wanted by her words alone. Women never knew what they really wanted. They only knew what they thought they wanted and the two were never, ever the same.

CHAPTER 3: SARAH

    Two evenings later Sarah waited in the interview room. Ethan had gone to get the next candidate. She'd interviewed one yesterday. It hadn't gone well. He'd seemed interested, but the way he'd looked at her had sent a shiver down her spine and not in a good way. So, she'd crossed him from her list and the rude man from the Viewing had dropped out. That left her with three. She glanced at the door. They should've been here by now. She hoped another candidate hadn't dropped out.

    Her lingerie photos had garnered considerable interest, but more than half had declined the next stage of the process because of her demands. These men were used to either getting their way with women or having women dominate them. Most weren't ready for a little of both. After she'd given Ethan her list of seven, he'd suggested she lower her standards, but she'd refused. She wanted a man she was attracted to and one who'd agree to her rules. Most on the original list of twenty-two fell short in either the appearance department or their portfolios had requirements in them that she wouldn't do.

The door opened and Ethan entered followed by another man. She'd seen his picture of course, but there was something smooth, sensual and dangerous about him. He almost glided into the room, confident and pure male.

"Sarah, this is Nicholas." Ethan placed a cell phone on the table between them. They were to call when they were done or if they needed anything. "I'll leave you to your discussion."

As long as he didn't drool or give her the creeps, this man would do. He'd do very nicely. He had dark hair and a slight tint to his skin, like he was of Italian or perhaps Greek descent. His eyes were so brown they were almost black and framed by a strong brow and thick, dark lashes she'd kill for. His body was lean and muscular, his arms well defined. He wore jeans and a polo. She'd expected a suit like the other man had worn. Clothes that'd accentuate his wealth and power. Her eyes skimmed down his legs as he sat.

"Is Sarah your real name," he asked.

"Yes. Is Nicholas yours?" This was the man with the voice; the one that'd sent tingles through her with his words.

"Yeah, but my friends call me Nick."

"Am I your friend?" Things were looking up. Maybe, she'd be successful after all. He was attractive, smelled nice and his voice made her body hum.

"That's what we're here to find out, isn't it?" His dark eyes seemed to caress her as they trailed from her face to her breasts.

Her nipples tightened as if it were his fingers, not his eyes touching them. Luckily, she'd worn the padded, push up bra. It wouldn't do to let him know he affected her so easily.

"A drink?" He stood and walked to the bar.

She shouldn't. She needed to keep her mind sharp. This was where they'd negotiate her demands and his to see if they'd come to an agreement, but she found herself saying, "Yes, thank you."

"Red or white?" He pointed to the wine.

"Crown Royale on the rocks."

His lips quirked upward as his eyes gleamed with surprise. He turned and poured her a healthy drink. He filled another glass with Glenlivet scotch straight and came back to the table.

"Thank you." She accepted the glass, her fingers brushing against his for a moment and a tingle ran straight to her belly and lower. As far as attraction went, he'd do very, very nicely.

He sat down across from her, leaning back in his chair. She took a sip, letting the liquor relax her. She hadn't been nervous with the other candidate because there'd been nothing for her to lose. She hadn't found him attractive, but this man...this man she wanted.

"Shall we start," he said.

"Of course. Sorry." She slid two contracts across the table. "I've already marked the options on your list that...won't work for me."

A thinning of his sensual lips was the only sign he was unhappy. She wanted to kiss him, remove his unhappiness. She took another drink. Perhaps, he wouldn't do after all. She didn't want to be too attracted to the man or she'd fall for him and she had no intention of doing that. One broken heart in a lifetime was enough.

"Let's see what you find so"—his eyes roamed over her again, making her skin tingle—"distasteful that it isn't even worth a discussion."

"Don't get angry. There aren't many things that…that I won't agree to try."

He flipped through the pages, stopping on his list of desires. His finger tapped the paper. "A threesome can be quite enjoyable."

"No. Only you and me for eight weeks." She didn't want two men or another woman. She wanted one man and her fantasies.

"Eight weeks is too long." He flipped through her contract, stopping on the page where she'd set the time limit and glancing up at her. "I'll grow tired of you before then."

Her back stiffened. That was rude, but this part was all about honesty. "How many weeks then? I'm flexible."

"I certainly hope so." He grinned.

That smile with the hidden meaning made more wetness pool between her legs. Too much time with this man would be dangerous. She didn't want to forget that this wasn't real. It was only a fantasy they'd create together.

"May I see you naked before I agree to a time limit?"

"You heard my rules the other night. I'll only undress for the one I choose."

His eyes hardened a bit. "And you haven't chosen

me yet."

"Exactly." She still had the polite man and another one to interview.

"Come here." He shifted his chair so it was facing away from the table.

"Why?" She wanted to obey, but she forced herself to remain seated.

"I'd like a better look at what you showed the other night. A closer look."

The throbbing between her legs made her shift on her seat. If she got too close and he touched her, she'd let him do anything. She wanted him that badly. She stood. "No touching."

He frowned but nodded.

She walked over to him, her hands shaking a little.

"Turn around."

She did as he commanded.

"Raise your skirt."

Her hands trembled as she gathered the cloth between her fists, slowly raising it to right below her butt.

"Higher, please." His voice was a whisper of desire that twisted in her stomach and settled between her thighs.

"That's as high as I went the other night." She wanted to raise her skirt all the way and sit on his lap, take him inside of her, but this wasn't the time. They still had a contract to go over.

"May I touch you." He'd leaned forward, his breath a heated caress at the small of her back. "Just where your skin is bare."

She shouldn't, but she nodded. She could swear she heard the smile in his exhale as his hand, rough and warm ran up her outer thigh and then down before sliding around to the back. His fingers trailed upward, this time on her inner thigh. It was a slow caress and she wanted to spread her legs to give him better access, but he stopped right at her skirt. Her heart pounded, wanting him to continue and his breathing was warm and ragged on her legs.

"Turn around."

His voice was barely a whisper but it may as well have been a command because there was no way she could disobey. When she turned, his face would be right where she wanted it.

She moved slowly, his hands keeping contact with her flesh. Her legs were trembling as she stood before him. He inhaled deeply. He had to know how aroused she was. He lifted his head, his eyes black with desire.

"Raise your skirt. You did the other night. Right before you dropped it."

Her heart was going to explode out of her chest. Sex wasn't part of this stage, she kept reminding herself but her hands moved upward. When her skirt was around her waist she stopped, glad she'd worn a sexy pair of panties. His eyes feasted on her mound as if he could see through the turquoise satin. His fingers moved upward on her thigh. He was so close to where she wanted him, so close to where she needed his touch, but this wasn't the time. Her breath hitched in her throat as she stepped back, dropping her skirt.

"I didn't say you could do that."

That was it. That was the reason they couldn't do this now. There was no contract and a man like him expected obedience that she wouldn't always give. "It's what I did the other night and it's all you get." She started toward her chair but he grabbed her wrist, stopping her.

"Your bra. I get to see that up close too."

She thought about refusing him, but the muscle twitching in his cheek told her he was on the edge and she was a little frightened and aroused by what would happen if she pushed him over. It might cause him to grab her and touch her and she wouldn't stop him. Then, he'd be her partner for the next several weeks and she'd obey every order he gave, or he might get mad and leave and she didn't want that.

She turned toward him and unbuttoned the first button on her blouse. His eyes raked in the exposed skin. She unhooked another and another until she could slip the cloth off her shoulder. He stared at her matching turquoise bra but it hid more than it exposed, except the top of her breasts. Those were for him to feast his eyes upon and he did. She glanced at the bulge in his pants. It was firm and long and her panties became uncomfortably wet.

"That's enough." She stepped back, starting to button her shirt.

"Leave it."

"We still have a lot to talk about."

"Please." His gaze met hers but even though the word was a request, his eyes demanded she obey.

She shrugged and moved back to her seat. Having him focus on her breasts might give her an edge in the negotiations. She sat, clearing her throat and straightening her contracts. "Do you want to go over the rest of what I won't agree to, or are you good?"

His lips quirked upward in a half smile. "Oh, I'm

very good but"—he tapped the page without looking at it—
"we need to agree on how long this contract will last or the
rest doesn't matter. My limit is usually a month, but I think
you'll be fun for a little longer. I'll agree to just the two of
us and to five weeks but not eight."

Five weeks was better than his usual month, but it
wasn't eight. That left her going back to her lonely bed
three weeks sooner. "I'll take that into consideration when
I make my choice."

"This is a negotiation. You're not supposed to hold
what we agree upon against me."

"Really? That's exactly what this stage is for. Yes,
it's a negotiation but I'm going to choose the man who is
the perfect fit."

"Come here and I'll prove that I fit perfectly." His
eyes gleamed.

"That's not what I meant." She wanted to do
exactly that. Instead, she shifted on her seat putting
pressure on her pussy. It was a poor substitute for his touch
but it was the best she had.

"Perhaps, but keep it in mind." He flipped through
the rest of the document. "The other dismissals are fine,
but not this one."

"Which one?" She leaned forward to see where he
was pointing. This was going better than she'd expected.
Of course, there hadn't been much that she'd taken off the
table. Most of the items she'd said she'd be willing to try
once. She could give him this one as a gift.

"I'm not using a condom."

"Oh," her mouth dropped open. She hadn't even
considered that it'd be a problem. "You have to."

"I'm clean and so are you. Ask Ethan. We're all tested."

"Yes, I know, but—"

"You're on birth control. So, what's the problem?"

It was true. Just one more perk from the La Petite Mort Club. The women were implanted with a device so pregnancy was highly unlikely. "They don't always work."

"They work. We'll be fine."

"No. Really. I did my research. No birth control is one hundred percent effective." She knew that for a fact.

"Neither are condoms."

"No, but the two together are closer." She wasn't going to budge on this.

"But not one hundred percent."

"Well, no, but..."

"Do you want me to fuck you through your underwear?"

"What? No. Is that even possible?"

"Fuck no, it's not possible but that's what a condom feels like."

"You have to use a condom." This was spiraling out of control. She really wanted this guy but she couldn't, wouldn't give on this point.

"I'll pay if you get pregnant." He jotted something on the paper. "Ethan will add it to our contract."

"Pay? For what? An abortion? Child support for the next twenty years?"

"Whatever you want?"

The arrogance of the man made her want to slap him. "And how much is a father worth to a child? How about my life that'd be turned upside down by raising your child alone?"

"You'd keep the baby?" His eyes raked over her face, studying her.

"Yes. No. I don't know." She leaned forward, forgetting about her unbuttoned shirt until his gaze settled on her breasts. She sat up, buttoning her shirt.

"Leave it. You agreed."

"That was before you started being an ass." She continued buttoning.

His lips narrowed but there was something in his eyes—amusement, respect, something besides desire. "Okay. I'll wear a condom, but you have to agree to discuss it during our time together." He leaned forward his eyes dropping to her breasts again. "One time may be worth the risk."

"Sure, when you're only risking money."

"Have you ever had a man come inside you?"

The ache between her legs started to throb again. She'd always used condoms. Everyone did, or at least she'd thought so.

"His release hot and wet shooting into you, filling you even more." He studied her. "It's an experience you shouldn't miss."

"I won't. I'm sure I'll marry one day."

"I'm surprised you're not married already." He studied her. "You're what, twenty-seven?"

She nodded. That information was all in the package.

"Why haven't you married?"

"That's none of your business."

He tipped his head in acknowledgment. Personal

matters were confidential. They weren't to know each other's last name, job, address, nothing. It was one of the rules of the club. They could only get that information if they both sent a request to Ethan four months after their contract was over. Otherwise, it'd stay sealed.

"So, you agree we can discuss the use of condoms during our evenings together."

"Yes." She jotted a note by that condition on her paper also. "However, I want you to know I won't change my mind."

"Challenge accepted." He grinned, as he tossed back his scotch. He tapped her glass as he stood. "Drink up."

She shouldn't but she did. She took two more swallows and handed him the empty glass. He made them both another drink and returned to the table.

He took a small sip and opened her contract. "Now, on to your demands." He glanced up at her, a smile in his eyes. "I'm sure I'll be happy to give you whatever you want and some things you don't even know you want."

"I know what I want."

He grinned in a way that clearly said she was clueless. She took another drink to keep from slapping that smirk off his face.

"Give me a minute to look this over." He studied the paper.

She took another drink as the liquor made a slow, warm path to her stomach. She watched him, wanting to go to him. He'd be willing. She could run her fingers through his thick, black hair as he lifted her skirt, his hands trailing up her thighs as he'd done before, exposing her to his eyes and his touch and his mouth with those lovely lips that promised pleasure.

CHAPTER 4: NICK

Nick opened Sarah's contract, laying it next to his and skimming over the section on what she would and wouldn't do. He loved that Ethan made both parties fill it out separately. That gave him a clearer picture of what she was interested in and comfortable with and how hard he'd have to work on each item to change her mind. "I noticed you had some "no's" on your sheet that you changed to "maybe" on mine."

"That's not uncommon in negotiations."

He almost laughed. He could write a book on negotiations. He was a very successful businessman but she didn't know that. "I just want to make sure where you stand."

"The items that I initially said "no" to are things I'm not interested in trying, but I'm willing to do it once if the man I choose really wants to."

"You mean me." He was getting annoyed with the *man I choose* crap. He wanted her and she wanted him. It should be done. He should be fucking her right now.

"I *mean* the man I choose. I haven't chosen you yet."

He was going to enjoy making her suffer for this. He'd bring her close to orgasm and stop, making her understand, just a little, how he was feeling right now. "Anal sex is something you're willing to try?"

"Yes, if you must have it."

"Have you ever been fucked in the ass?"

"No." She squirmed in her seat.

She liked it when he talked dirty. His dick, already hard, hardened even more at the thought of being inside her when she squirmed like that. He was glad Ethan had called him about this one. He'd been going to pass on attending the Viewing. She wasn't that interesting on paper, but Ethan had pushed and, as usual, had been right. She was fascinating in person. "You may find you enjoy it."

"Perhaps, but it isn't something I really want to try."

"Why not? It's good to add to your arsenal of pleasure."

"I suppose, but"—she wrinkled her nose a little—"I don't think I'll get any pleasure out of it."

"You would've said the same thing about a man fucking your cunt when you were a virgin and you would've been wrong."

Her brow raised in challenge and she glanced down at his contract. "Have you tried pegging? I noticed you marked that as a firm no."

Touché. "No." He shifted, trying to give his cock some room in his, now, very tight pants. He'd never imagined a conversation could be so arousing.

"Perhaps we should add that to the list. You may find you enjoy it and I've always been curious about the double-sided dildos." She made that adorable face again where she wrinkled her pert, little nose. "I don't quite see how the rhythm would work."

"We are not adding it to the list. You marked no and so did I. It's off the table." He wasn't going to let anyone fuck him in the ass, no matter how hot she was.

"Fine." She struggled to stop her grin. "Then anal sex is off the table too."

"You agreed it was a maybe," he said. She was really starting to annoy him.

"I've changed my mind. The contract hasn't been signed yet."

"Fine." He tossed back the rest of his drink. She was a piece of work. Unfortunately, that made him want her more. "Next topic. I noticed that me coming in your mouth was a maybe on both lists."

"Yes." She straightened slightly as a slight blush painted her cheeks.

"Have you ever done that before?"

"No."

"But you want to?

"Yes, I'd like to try it. I may puke though so you might want to save that for the end of the evening."

"I'll make sure to eat a lot of pineapple before the big day."

Her eyebrows scrunched up in confusion.

"My cum will taste better if I eat pineapple or blueberries." He paused. "At least that's what I've heard."

"You've never done this either?"

"Oh, I've done it, but I've never tasted my own cum."

"Oh, right. Of course." Her face heated even more.

"Don't be embarrassed. We're going to be very, very intimate. You don't need to ever be embarrassed around me."

"*We* may not be doing anything."

He clenched his teeth. This was past old. "Of course. You haven't chosen yet." He looked back at the paper. "What is it about being fucked in the ass that you dislike?"

"I thought we were done with this topic." She squirmed again.

"We would be your body tells me you're getting more than turned on by the discussion." And quite frankly so was he. He'd been in these interviews before and had never gotten so hard. The jeans were a poor decision, not much room for growth.

"I'm not—"

"Don't lie. You're squeezing your legs together to put pressure on your pussy."

"How?" Her eyes widened as she forced her legs apart a little, shifting in her seat again.

"By the way you sit and squirm. I'll be gentle and I'll make it good."

"I am turned on, but not because I'm anticipating being fucked in the ass."

"Anticipation of what then? Sucking my dick. We can remedy all of this—"

"Having sex again."

"With me."

"Right now, yes, but in the next interview it may be him that I'm anticipating fucking."

"I don't get jealous so don't try." He was annoyed though. She needed to choose him and she needed to do it before the next interview.

"I'm not trying to make you jealous. I'm being honest."

"Why are you here doing this?"

"I want to be fucked."

"A woman like you should be able to do that without the help and expense of this club."

"It takes time to date and find someone."

"You could pick a guy up in any bar who'd be more than willing to take you any way you want."

"That's not safe. This has a level of protection the other means don't."

He tipped his head in acknowledgement of that statement.

"Can we continue?" She looked at her watch. "I have to leave soon."

She didn't have time for him. That was a first and it wasn't pleasant. He tossed back his drink and went to the bar, this time bringing both bottles and the ice bucket back to the table. He filled her glass and then his before sitting and looking back at the contract.

"Of course, I wouldn't want to keep you…from whatever you have to do."

She sighed. "Don't be a baby. We both have lives outside—"

"No. No. This won't work." He couldn't believe he'd missed this.

"What?" She scanned her document, glancing at his to see where he was pointing.

"Once a week? We're only to meet once a week?" He shook his head. He liked to fuck his women every day, several times a day, the first week and sometimes the second. After that it dwindled down to three to four times a week, but never once a week.

"Oh." She leaned back in her chair. "Sorry, but I can't budge on that one."

"That one? You haven't budged on any."

"That's not tr—"

"It doesn't matter. There is no way we're only going to meet once a week." He almost stood, but picked up his drink instead. "That won't be enough for me."

"You could agree to the eight nights."

"Eight nights in two months?" He leaned forward. She was unbelievable. He scratched through her requirement on her contract and his. "Every night for the first two weeks and then—"

"I'm sorry. I can't." She gave him a sad smile. "I wish I could but I can't get away that often."

"You aren't married. Ethan's background checks are better than the government's and he said you're single."

"I am single."

"I don't understand. Do you have kids?"

"That's none of your business."

She was right and it irritated him even more. He itched to walk over there, pull her to her feet and push her down against the table and fuck her good and hard. Show her he was in charge, but he stayed where he was and finished his drink. "Why can't you get away?"

"That's also personal and none of your business. This was a firm requirement and it was in the dossier from the beginning."

It was and he'd missed it. He hadn't been interested until she'd told Terry "no" and then when he'd seen the eight weeks he hadn't paid any attention to what was written below it. "Too bad. I can't agree to this." It was her move.

She frowned and sighed, making her breasts press against her shirt and his mouth water. She'd taste sweet and a little tangy, he was sure.

"I'm sorry. I really am." She reached across the table. She was going to call his bluff, call Ethan and end this interview.

He snatched the phone from under her hand. "Don't bother. I'll go get him." He stormed from the room. She was going to refuse him. Let him walk away. That was fine. He didn't need her either. He grabbed one of the girls, who was chatting in the hallway, by the hand. He needed to fuck someone right now. "Come with me."

She obeyed, trailing after him into one of the bedrooms. He pulled out his wallet and handed her a wad of bills before shoving his wallet back into his pants. She was short and blonde and buxom with cherry red lips that screamed "I want to suck your cock." He pushed her against the door and started to shove her skirt out of his way when someone knocked.

"Nick, is the interview done?" asked Ethan. "You know the rules if you're dropping out. You haven't signed the forms to give up your place."

"Go the fuck away, Ethan. I'll sign the damn forms

32

later."

"Are you sure about this? She's one of a kind."

He rested his head against the girl's breasts and inhaled deeply. Ethan was right. He could have a hundred girls like this one, any day, any time. They'd do whatever he said, but Sarah was different. He couldn't bully her and that made him want to fuck her into submission. He pulled out his wallet again and gave the girl some more money. "Next time, honey."

He walked into the hallway.

"So, what'd she do to piss you off this much?" asked Ethan as they headed back to the interview room.

"We're only to meet once a week."

"That was in the contract." Ethan shot him a sideways glance.

"No shit. I missed it. You should've told me. I never would've bothered with the Viewing." If he'd never met her, he'd never miss not stripping her bare and making her beg and scream for him.

"Isn't it better to fuck her brains out for eight nights than for none?"

He shrugged. "You have a point."

"Just make those nights count."

"I'll make sure she can't walk when we're done." He'd fuck her every way he could imagine and he had a very good imagination.

Ethan slapped him on the back. "Go and nail...this interview."

"Oh, I'll be nailing more than that." He walked back into the room.

CHAPTER 5: SARAH

Sarah stared at the closed door. She shouldn't be so disappointed. Nick wouldn't be good for her. She wanted him too much. So much her mind was scrambling, trying to figure out a way to meet him more than once a week, but it was impossible. Lisa was only available Saturdays and she couldn't, she wouldn't leave Tank for hours with someone else.

Tank had been Adam's dog in the military. He'd sniffed out IEDs until he'd been injured in the same gunfire that'd killed Adam. She gathered the papers together. She still had two more men to interview. One of them would do, but she didn't want someone who'd do. She wanted Nick.

She sipped her drink, hoping Nick would return and agree to her conditions but if anyone asked, she was waiting for Ethan to make Nick's withdrawal official. She finished her drink and poured another. One more but that was it. She had to drive.

The door opened and Nick stormed inside followed by Ethan. Nick was furious, his black eyes almost blazing as a muscle twitched in his cheek. Even angry she wanted him. She wanted to go to him and offer herself to ease his temper. He was definitely not good for her.

"Six nights. Day and time of my choosing." Nick stood by his chair, hands clasping the top so hard his knuckles were white. "And I can see other women the rest of the week."

"That seems reasonable." Ethan shot her an encouraging look.

"It is but I can't."

Nick's face hardened even more and he spun around.

"I can only meet on Saturdays. You pick the time, but it has to be Saturday." She was pleading but she couldn't help herself. He wouldn't come back if he left again.

He turned around and moved back to the table. "We sign the papers right now. No more interviews. You choose me." He almost growled the last word.

She nodded. She was doomed by this attraction, but warmth pooled in her belly. It'd be a glorious time…until it wasn't.

Nick's eyes drifted down her face to her breasts. Her nipples immediately hardened and the warmth in her belly moved lower, causing wetness to gather between her thighs. She squeezed them together a little, to feel the pressure, find a little relief from the aching emptiness. His lips turned upward in a half-smirk. He must have noticed her movement. The heat flooded her face too.

"Great. Let's get these papers signed." Ethan pulled a blank contract from his jacket and filled it out as he flipped through their original contracts.

Nick filled his glass with more scotch and started to pour her another, but she put her hand over the top of the glass. He raised his brow, daring her to defy him again.

"I have to drive."

"Get an Uber."

"No. I'd have to get another one to come back for my car and…No."

"I think the first thing we'll do is teach you the word yes." He sat across from her.

"I know that word too, but for some reason you make me say the other one much more." She smiled.

"We'll work on changing that."

"I've added the conditions and preferences from each of your contracts to this one." Ethan handed the papers to her. "Look it over and sign on the bottom of the last page."

She read it and signed.

Ethan slid it across the table to Nick who read it and signed.

"That's that then." Ethan gathered the contract. "Nick will send me the details for your meetings—location, time, etc and I'll forward it to you." He turned to her. "Since this is your first time, I'll go over the process verbally if you like? It's all in the papers, but"—he grinned—"who really reads contracts."

"Yes, please do." She fidgeted under Nick's dark gaze.

"The only contact the two of you will have, except

on the day and time detailed in the contract, will be, must be, coordinated through me. If you decide you want him to wear or bring something special that you didn't speak with him about during your session, you must let me know at least a day in advance. We prefer three days, but we'll do our best with short notice. If you need to cancel—"

"That had better not happen." Nick's voice was a rumbled warning.

Ethan shot him a glare. "If you need to cancel due to illness or emergency, contact me as soon as possible. I'll need documentation to verify—"

"Like a doctor's note?" she asked. He had to be kidding.

"Yes." Ethan's eyes were serious. "This is a binding contract." The friendly, businessman had disappeared, replaced by a dangerous man until he smiled again. "If there's a real reason to cancel, it's okay, but don't jerk me around."

Nick snorted. "You'd better be in the hospital if you cancel."

"That's not necessary." Ethan held up his hand to shut Nick up. "Let me continue or we'll be here all night."

Nick nodded slightly and took a drink.

"As I was saying, don't cancel unless you absolutely have to. Okay?"

"I hadn't planned on cancelling." If she cancelled she'd have to stay at home with Lisa and she didn't think she could do that. She still hated the other woman for taking Adam from her.

"Good. If after the first night, you realize things aren't...good between the two of you, you may cancel the contract. I'll retain fifty percent of the fee from the person who cancelled and twenty percent from the other party."

"Wow. Fifty percent." That was a lot of money for a one night fling but Nick didn't even flinch. Of course, he was rich. He had to be to afford the membership to the club. Her one-time fee had almost given her heart palpitations. She didn't even want to think about what a yearly membership would cost.

"You're both adults. You both agreed to this. I've invested a lot of time and money in this transaction."

"I wasn't aware that I could cancel so, it's fine."

"You'll have no reason to." Nick's eyes were blazing hot as he studied her. "Things will be very, very good between us."

"That about sums it up," said Ethan. "Remember, all communication must be done through me."

She nodded. Everything personal was off limits anyway, so that worked fine for her.

"Good. I'm off to file these." Ethan grabbed the papers and left.

She stood.

"Where do you think you're going?" Nick leaned back in his chair, his eyes on her breasts.

"Ah, we're done for the night." The smooth calmness in his voice sent a tingle down her spine. He was like a predator waiting to pounce and she was all alone, helpless.

"There is one thing in your dossier we have yet to do."

"I don't recall..." And then she did. She'd insisted on having one kiss from each interviewee. "We were supposed to do that before we signed." She'd goofed but she was pretty sure he wasn't a lousy kisser. "We can skip that."

"No, we can't." He scooted his chair away from the table. "Come here."

She didn't move, afraid one kiss wouldn't be all he'd take and she didn't know if she had the will to stop him.

"I won't tell you again." His gaze locked with hers, making it clear that next time he'd make her.

She moved over to him, her body tensing with excitement and fear. This man was dangerous and it thrilled her. She stopped in front of him and in a quick second he lifted her and set her on the table.

"Oh," she squeaked as his hands wandered up her legs, caressing from calf to knee to thigh. "That's...that's not a kiss." She wasn't sure why she said it – to stop him or to challenge him.

He took it as a challenge as he smiled and lowered his face to her leg.

"Oh." It was all she could say again as he trailed open mouth kisses up her thighs, pushing her skirt out of his way as he went.

He grabbed her legs, pulling her to the edge of the table, and shoved her thighs apart as his mouth continued to kiss and lick and suck. Her hands went to his hair, pulling him closer and he nipped the smooth, soft skin of her inner thigh. It was unexpected and a little painful, but her legs spread wider giving him more room as she shifted, a little, toward his face and those lips and that wonderful mouth. He stopped right below her pussy. She pushed his head closer and he smiled against her leg before blowing across her aching flesh. She moaned, arching her back and offering herself to him. He was going to make her come just by promise. He blew on her again. She wanted more than that. It was insubstantial, temporary. She wanted his lips and tongue.

"Please." She tugged his face closer, her hands tangling in his thick, soft hair.

He ran his finger along her cunt and she shivered. His touch was hard and it felt so good but then his hand was gone. He sat up, moving away from her and leaning against the back of his chair.

"What? No, please." She wanted to slap her hand over her mouth. She never begged, not anymore, but she couldn't help it. She was so close. All he needed to do was touch her a few more times and she'd find her release.

"I'll see you Saturday." He tossed back his drink and stood.

"Why? Why did you…"

"Stop?"

She nodded.

"Because you needed to be taught a lesson."

"A lesson?" She tugged her skirt down, covering her underwear.

"Yes. I gave more on that contract than I should've."

"I didn't make you." She stood. This man was too much. Too arrogant. Too confident. Too much of an asshole.

"And I didn't make you come, but I did make you beg." His eyes sparkled and his words hit her like a punch to the gut.

"It won't happen again."

He laughed. "Oh, you'll be begging me every Saturday."

"No. I won't because I have twenty-four hours to change my mind." She smiled. "Seems I only needed a few minutes. I doubt Ethan's even had time to cancel the other interviews."

As she walked past him, his arm snaked around her waist, yanking her against his hard body for one second before her feet left the floor and she was back on the table, this time lying down with Nick leaning over her.

"You are not changing your mind." His mouth came down on hers, hard and forceful.

She shoved at his chest. She didn't want it like this and then he nipped her lips and she gasped, giving way for his tongue. He thrust into her mouth and she moaned, her hands trailing up his back to his hair, pulling him closer. He grabbed her legs, tugging her down to the edge of the table and pushing her skirt up. She gasped as he raised her legs, wrapping them around his waist. His erection rubbed against her, hard and long as his tongue thrust into her mouth. She rocked against him. She'd missed this. She'd missed this so much. His hand came up and started unbuttoning her blouse but after a moment, he became impatient and tore them loose. Buttons hit the table and his mouth moved to her breast, above her bra.

She pushed herself into him, rubbing and rocking against his hardness, wetness soaking her panties. She needed this. She needed him. She was so close. He freed her breast and he sucked hard on her nipple. She moaned as she came, her release racing through body. He rocked against her, keeping her orgasm going a moment or two longer.

Her body finally settled and a feeling of lassitude filled her. Her bones were liquid but he was still hard between her legs. He unzipped his pants and a tingle of excitement sparked to life again.

"Oh, oh...I'm so sorry," said a female voice.

He pushed off her and spun around. A young girl in a maid's uniform stood by the door, her brown eyes filled with surprise.

"Get the hell out of here," he yelled.

"I'm sorry. Ethan said you were done." The maid tugged on the cleaning cart in front of her. "I clean the rooms after..." Her eyes darted to Sarah, her red face getting even redder.

That's when she realized she was still lying on the table, breasts out, skirt above her waist with her legs spread. "Oh, my god," she whispered as she jumped off the table and darted toward the door, tucking her breasts back into her bra.

"Sarah, stop."

The command in Nick's voice made her step falter but embarrassment spurred her on. "See you Saturday," she yelled as she pushed past the cart, shoving it out of her way, and darted around the girl and out the door.

"Sarah! Get back here!"

This time his command made her legs move faster. If he caught her, they'd have sex and she wasn't ready for that. Not with him, not with anyone who wasn't Adam. She hiked up her skirt and ran. As soon as she made it into the administration wing—to the room where she'd left her things and had waited for Ethan to escort her into the club—she slammed the door, breathing heavily. Nick wasn't allowed in this section of the club. This was for visitors, one time buyers, and Nick was a member. She turned the lock just in case he didn't follow the rules. She buttoned her shirt, her fingers fumbling in her haste, giving up when she realized that most of the buttons were gone. She unlocked the locker, grabbed her purse, clenched her shirt together and fled into the attached garage.

She was glad he hadn't followed, truly she was. He was probably fucking the little maid, but that was okay because they weren't in a relationship. She had him for six nights. That'd be enough, more than enough.

She got into her car and breathed easy for the first time since he'd entered the interview room. Then she remembered the look on his face as she'd darted out the door, leaving him rock hard and furious. She couldn't blame him. She was an adult and adults didn't run away after having an orgasm, especially leaving their partner— no he wasn't her partner, Adam had been her partner—their sex-partner unfulfilled. She wouldn't blame him if he cancelled. He also had twenty-four hours to change his mind. Part of her hoped he would. That'd be easier because otherwise sometime between today and Saturday she had to get ready to have sex with someone who wasn't Adam.

CHAPTER 6: SARAH

Sarah sat in her car, staring at the paper in her hand. Room nineteen-twelve at the Hilton at nine o'clock. She'd been relieved and disappointed a few days ago when she'd received Nick's note from Ethan. She'd been sure Nick would cancel their contract after her embarrassing exit the day of the interview.

She glanced at her watch. Ten after nine. She needed to go, to meet Nick for…sex. She took a deep breath and got out of her car. She entered the lobby and headed for the elevator. This was what she'd wanted, needed. It was just sex. Physical relief. *Yeah, with a stranger.* But there was nothing wrong with that. They were both consenting adults. This did not make her a whore.

The elevator doors opened and she stepped inside, pressing the nineteen. Her stomach was in knots and she wasn't even a little sexually excited. This whole thing was a mistake. She'd never had sex with a stranger. She'd only had sex with one other man, boy really, besides Adam.

The elevator stopped on her floor and she got out and headed for the room. Adam had been her high school sweetheart. They'd started dating at fifteen and hadn't broken up until he'd gone into the service and she'd gone to college. She'd wanted to stay together, but Adam had insisted that it was better to break up. That's when she'd had sex with Stephen. It'd only been a couple of times and it hadn't been great. She'd been in love with Adam and no one could replace him. Her hand froze before knocking on the door. Would this be not great too? She was still in love with Adam. It didn't matter that he'd been dead for six years, she still loved him. This wouldn't change that. This was just physical and it was the only opportunity she'd have for a while. Plus, she'd agreed to it. She choked on a laugh. Not only had she agreed, she'd signed a bloody contract. She knocked before she could change her mind.

Nick opened the door, stepping aside so she could enter. "You're late."

He had a drink in hand, probably scotch and was dressed in jeans and a plain white T-shirt. The casual clothes made him seem more approachable and yet more male. More working class, the kind of guys she'd grown up with.

He shut the door behind her and walked across the room. His ass looked nice in the jeans and some of her nervousness was pushed away by desire.

He sat on the couch and his eyes raked over her body. "Take off your clothes. Slowly."

"What? Now?" She'd figured they'd talk a little, work up to this.

"Yes. Now. This isn't a date." He took a sip of his drink.

"I...I know that." She did but still she wasn't a prostitute although the only difference was she wasn't getting paid.

"I've waited days. You on the other hand had an orgasm a few days ago. I did not."

"Ah, yeah, sorry about that." She didn't blame him for being upset. She'd acted like a child but what if he were really angry?

"Just take off your clothes."

Her hands trembled so much as she tried to unbutton her shirt that she couldn't get a hold of the button. This wasn't what she'd wanted. She didn't need or want the boyfriend experience but she had to work up to sex. She dropped her hands. "Can't we talk a bit? I'll get a drink—"

"No." In a second he was in front of her.

He towered over her—this stranger who she was alone with, who she'd promised to have sex with in numerous ways. She wasn't ready. She may never be ready. "I'm sorry...I can't." She took a step back and he grabbed her arm.

"Oh no. You aren't getting away again." He yanked her to him and his arms went around her, grabbing her ass and pulling her into him, into his erection which was already hard and growing. "You agreed to this. You could've backed out earlier. You're not backing out now. Tonight, you're mine and I can do whatever I want with you."

She trembled as his lips found her neck. She tried

to relax but couldn't. He was a stranger and he was stronger than her. The contract didn't matter. He could do whatever he wanted and she couldn't stop him.

He stopped kissing her and loosened his hold, giving her reprieve from his body. "Jesus, you're really scared." He sounded surprised.

"I...I'm sorry." She was. She'd wanted this and it wasn't his fault.

"Come here." He took her hand and led her to the couch. "Sit."

He went and poured her a drink, Crown on the rocks, and himself another scotch. He came back, handing her the glass and sitting sideways on the couch so he could see her. He was close but not too close.

"I thought you were role playing." He studied her face. His desire banked but the flames still flickered in his gaze. "I love fucking women when they're pretending to be frightened. I play the master, boss, lord of the manor or whatever you want to call it well, but I don't fuck women who are actually afraid. Understand?"

She nodded and took a large gulp of her drink, coughing a little. "I'm sorry. Really, I am."

"You've never done this have you?"

"I've had sex but never with a stranger."

He nodded as he took another drink, his eyes never leaving her and making her a little uncomfortable. "Maybe, I should call Ethan."

"No." Panic clawed at her chest. If she didn't go through with this now, she never would. "I still want to..." She waved her hand.

His eyebrows raised.

She couldn't blame him for not believing her. She wasn't acting like a woman who wanted sex. "Maybe if we talked a little first."

He leaned against the arm of the couch. "I'm not sure what we can talk about. Everything personal is off limits."

She had to think of something or he'd leave. He didn't strike her as the kind of man to wait too long for something. "Do you like animals?" It was all she could think of and if he did like animals he couldn't be all bad.

"Yeah, I guess."

"Do you have any pets?" It was a personal question but not too personal. No one was going to be able to find someone online by knowing if they had pets.

"No. I don't have time for pets."

"Oh." She couldn't imagine life without Tank, although he was getting older and soon he'd be gone along with Adam and their baby. "You never had a pet?" She felt bad for the little boy he'd been.

"I did when I was a kid. We had this mutt, a mix of lord only knows what. He was huge and the biggest baby." He smiled but he wasn't looking at her, he was looking at his memories. "He was my best friend. We did everything together."

He blinked and cleared his throat, as if embarrassed by his emotion. She was glad he'd shared that little bit. She knew him better now, not much but a little and she relaxed.

"I've answered your questions and gave you a peek into my past." His eyes darkened as they trailed over her breasts. "Now, it's your turn."

"Okay. Ask me anything you want. I'll answer if I can."

His eyes snapped to her face. "I don't have any questions for you. I want to see you naked. I want to fuck you."

"Oh." She tried to hide her disappointment, but must have failed.

"Okay. Fine. We'll play your game, but we'll change the rules a bit."

"What rules?" This hadn't been a game but the idea of making it one had desire sparking to life throughout her body.

"I answered your question. Now, you take off an item of clothing."

Her face heated and she took another gulp of liquor to give her courage. She could play this game. She wanted to play this game. "And when I answer your questions, you'll take off an item of clothing."

"I'll strip bare right now if you'd like, but sure, we can do it through questions."

"Okay." She leaned over and removed her shoe. She dropped the sandal on the floor a few inches away.

"Really? Your shoes." He shook his head. "I'd ask you to leave them for last. I love seeing a woman in high heels and lingerie but those shoes..." He shivered. "Burn them."

She laughed. "They aren't that bad."

"They're flat." He stared at them with disgust.

"I can't walk in high heels."

"Shame." He moved in front of her, sitting on the coffee table. "Amendment to the rule. I get to remove your clothes and you get to remove mine."

Her heart kicked up its pace and desire curled in her belly. She'd be able to touch him, his hard chest and arms and more. "Okay, but I'm done for this round."

"Oh, no." He took her still shoed foot in his hand. "Shoes come in pairs, like pants."

"Pants don't come in pairs."

"They're called a pair of pants." His long fingers skimmed her calf, massaging and sending more heat shooting through her and pooling between her thighs.

"Yeah, but you can't take off only part." She didn't care about the shoe, but sparring with him was turning her on.

"You could take off one leg. It'd be awkward and uncomfortable, but it could be done." He pulled her shoe from her foot. "We need to agree that pairs come off on one turn."

"Okay." She couldn't take her eyes from his dark head, focusing on her foot. His fingers massaged and she moaned softly, shifting against the couch a little. It'd been years since she'd had a foot rub as a prelude to sex. She hadn't even realized she'd missed this, but she had. Her leg rested on his strong thigh and his fingers pressed into muscles that seemed to be directly attached to her pussy, making it wet and needy.

He kissed the sole of her foot and moved back to the couch, his jeans a little tighter across the front than before. "Do you like animals?"

"Yes. What do you want me to remove?"

His lips twitched. "Not my shoes, darling."

Her gaze dropped to the button on his pants.

"Not those either. Not yet."

She raised her eyes, meeting his. Amusement warred with desire. She was sure she had the same look.

"My shirt." He leaned more firmly against the side of the couch.

She knelt on the cushion and moved toward him. Her hands went to the bottom of his T-shirt and she slowly lifted, her thumbs trailing up his torso. He was so warm and firm. She wanted to bend and let her lips follow her fingers, but then the game would be over and she was having fun.

He raised his arms and she pulled the shirt over his head, her breasts brushing against his chest, causing her to inhale sharply. His hand touched her back, holding her against him for a moment as his eyes locked with hers. His desire was raging. Her gaze dropped to his lips and his hands moved to her blouse.

She shifted away, but not far. "You have to answer a question first."

He smiled and she knew she'd missed something. The game was over and he'd won. "I answered three questions already."

"No, you—"

"Do you like animals, got me your shoes. Do you have any pets—what is that going to get me?" His gazed raked over her breasts like fingers.

She squeezed her thighs together, a poor substitute for the touch she really wanted. "Okay. You're right. You can have my shirt."

He took his time with each button, letting his fingers brush against her bared flesh for a quick, hot moment. Her heart pounded as she sat next to him on the couch, her feet tucked under her. He undid the last button and she shrugged helping him to remove the shirt, which he tossed on the floor by her shoes.

"You wore the green, thank you." His breathing was getting shallower and the heat coming from him made her want to lean into him to absorb his warmth, absorb him.

"You told me to." The color of her lingerie had been in the message she'd received with the location and time."

"Yes, but you could've disobeyed." His eyes raised to her for the first time since he'd started removing her shirt. "You seem to like doing that." His lips twitched with amusement and his eyes sparkled in challenge.

"It's good for you." She smiled back at him.

His eyes narrowed slightly, but there was still humor in them. "I prefer obedience."

This was fun. Sexy and fun. "I'm sure you do, but not always getting your way is good for you. I swear. It'll help you build character."

"I have enough character." His eyes dropped back to her breasts. "What are you going to give me for, did you ever have pets?"

That was a no brainer. "My skirt." She got off the couch and stood in front of him, turning around. Her breathing hitched as his hand trailed up her leg and over her ass to the zipper. God, she was wet, dripping. The sound of the zipper coming down filled the room and the cloth slid down her legs, making her shiver.

"Turn around." His voice was thick and heavy.

She turned and a wave of pure lust burst through her

at the hard desire on his face. She wanted him. She wanted this. She was done with the game. "Do you want me?"

His eyes shot to her face. "Of course, I want you." He glanced down at the huge bulge in his pants. "Painfully so."

"For that question, you get my bra."

Desire sparked and consumed his gaze, as he reached for her.

"No." She shifted away from his grasp. "Let me."

He leaned against the couch, his cock straining at his pants and his eyes on her breasts as she unclasped her bra. She held it, concealing herself for a moment before dropping it with her other clothes. "Do you have a question for me?" She wanted him naked.

It took him a moment to realize what she was asking and then his eyes lowered to the juncture of her thighs. "Are you wet?"

"Soaked. Does that make you happy?"

He kicked off his shoes and socks before standing, his chest almost touching hers. "Yes."

She hesitated at removing her underwear, her hands shaking for the first time in several minutes. Removing this was removing the last barrier between them.

He leaned closer to her and whispered in her ear, his hot breath causing her to shiver. "Do you want me to kiss you?"

She turned her face so their lips were only a hair's breadth away. "Yes."

And his mouth was on hers, hard and firm, coaxing her to open to him and she did. He pulled her close, pushing his tongue into her mouth and her hands wrapped around him, settling in his hair, holding him to her. He deepened the kiss, each thrust of his tongue making her pussy clench, wanting the same attention. His hands roamed her body, seeming to be everywhere at once—her ass, her back, her breasts. She pressed against him, trying to get as close as possible. His lips left her mouth to trail kisses down her face to her neck. This was what she'd wanted, dreamt about. He sucked on a sensitive spot on her neck and her back arched pushing herself against his hardness. He moved farther down, his mouth hot and wet as it came closer and closer to her breasts. Her nipples were puckered, begging for him. She thrust forward as his tongue, rough and hot, circled her nipple before his mouth came down hard, sucking and flicking with his tongue. Her knees buckled but his strong arms kept her on her feet, pressed against him. His mouth moved to her other breast as his hand skimmed along her ass, rubbing her against his erection. She lifted her leg, wrapping it around him. She had to get closer. She needed him closer. He grasped her thigh and pushed it down as he bent, kissing his way southward until he was kneeling before her. He gripped her thighs and stared up at her, his eyes dark with desire. Her legs trembled in anticipation and she steadied herself with her hands in his thick hair.

He kissed her hip bone and then a quick, hard kiss to her mound. She twitched, pushing her pussy toward his face. She was so close already. It'd only take another touch or two and she'd come.

"Please," she said, unable to find any other words.

He ignored her, pulling her underwear down her

hips, slowly, as he kissed and licked his way down one leg. She stepped out of the panties and he tossed them aside, his hot, wet mouth and tongue kissing its way up her other thigh. His hand tugged on her leg, lifting it.

"I…I can't, I'll fall." She had terrible balance on a good day, but today her legs were barely keeping her up as it was.

He lifted her, his hands under her ass and turned, placing her on the couch. He pulled her forward and raised her legs to his shoulders. She tried to calm down, enjoy the sensations but she knew as soon as he kissed her…there, it'd be over. She was too desperate for his touch. She leaned back her head, waiting as he gave wet, opened mouthed kisses up her thigh. He was almost there. So close but then he stopped.

"Look at me."

She leaned up on her elbows and trembled at his dark, lust filled face. His cheeks were hard like a statue's – a hot, strong, aroused statue. His eyes held hers as he kissed her inner thigh, his tongue flicking only centimeters away from where she wanted him. He turned his head and breathed across her cunt. She whimpered. She didn't want air or hot breath, she wanted his mouth, lips, tongue all of it. She shifted her pelvis upward and one side of his mouth quirked upward.

"Eager, aren't we?"

She should be embarrassed but she wasn't. She didn't care what he thought only what he did. "Yes, please Nick. Please."

He clasped her ass, holding her tight as he ran his tongue between her pussy lips. She moaned, closing her eyes and tipping back her head. He licked her again, this time, running his tongue over her little bud and her body twitched. She was close. So very close.

"Do you like that?" The hot breath from his words made her whimper.

"Yes. Please…again."

"Hold yourself open for me."

She leaned up on her elbows. "What?"

"If you want more, you'll have to help." His finger caressed her, soft strokes and then pressing for one exquisite second on her clit. "I'm serious. I'll stop if you—"

"Don't stop." She reached between her legs and spread her pussy lips wide.

"That's my girl." He lowered his face and his hot, wonderful tongue was back, licking and flicking.

She squirmed but his grip tightened, holding her still as his tongue thrust inside of her, over and over. She moaned and her hands moved to his hair, holding him in place. "Oh, oh, yes."

He stopped and she opened her eyes, staring at him in confusion.

"You have to help if you want me to continue."

"What?"

He moved one of her hands off his head, kissing her palm. "Hold yourself open for me."

"Oh. Right. Sorry." She spread her lower lips, displaying herself like a feast.

"If you move your hands again, I'll stop for good."

She'd die if he did that. Her body was a tight bundle of nerves. She needed release.

"Do you understand?"

"Yes." She squirmed a little, hoping he'd get back to business.

He grinned before lowering his head. He licked her again and again. Up one side and then the other. It was great but he kept missing her little bud and she really needed him there.

"Please, Nick." Her pelvis rocked toward him.

He took the hint and his mouth moved to her clit, his tongue twirling around it while he slipped one finger inside of her.

"Fuck, you're tight." He said against her pussy, his words sending vibrations through her as his finger thrust inside of her.

She moaned, rocking against his hand. He added another finger, stretching her. It felt so good and then he hooked his fingers, hitting a spot inside of her that almost made her leap off the couch. His other hand came down on her abdomen, holding her in place as he did it again and again. She thrashed under his hold. It was too much, too good. She couldn't stand it and when his lips locked on her clit and he sucked, she shot straight into orgasm. She bucked against his face, but he kept sucking and finger fucking her until her orgasm subsided. He kissed her one more time on her inner thigh and then stood, removing his pants.

She was too tired to move, so she stayed as she was—legs spread, half off and half on the couch. She felt better than she'd ever felt but the sight of his fully engorged penis made a trickle of apprehension flare to life. He was big, a lot bigger than the dildo she'd been using.

He tore open a condom and rolled it onto his dick. As soon as that was done, he grabbed her legs and shifted her so she was completely on the couch. He climbed on top of her and she tensed. His dick lay thick and heavy against her thigh. This wasn't going to feel good, but she couldn't stop. Not now. He held her head and thrust his tongue into her mouth, the games were over, the flirtation over. Desire ran too hot inside of him. He shoved her legs apart and shifted into position, his cock pushing at her entrance.

"Relax," he whispered in her ear.

"I'm trying."

"Try harder." There was a desperate edge to his voice.

"I can't relax just because you tell me to."

He nipped her ear and her pelvis shifted upward, as he pushed inside of her. He wasn't in very far, but she already felt stretched. His mouth moved to her neck, finding a sensitive spot. She moaned first from pleasure and then from pain as he slammed the rest of the way inside of her. He lay there, his breath hot and heavy against her ear.

"Finish, please." She wanted this done. He was too big or she was too tight. Either way, it hurt but it should be over soon.

He leaned up, the strain on his face making her feel bad. He was trying to make it good for her, but it wouldn't be. It'd only been good with Adam.

"It's okay. Just finish." She averted her eyes. This wasn't his fault.

He brushed the hair off her face and his lips touched hers gently as his tongue slipped into her mouth. She could taste herself on him and desire sparked again. He deepened the kiss, coaxing her to kiss him back and before she knew it, her arms were wrapped around him, her hands holding his head as her tongue sparred with his. This man could kiss. And then he moved, below, just a little. Out and then in.

"How's that feel? Still hurt?"

"No." She wasn't lying. It didn't hurt. Her body had gotten used to his size.

He moved again, a little more. More out and more in. Again and again. It felt good. She thrust against him, her desire building.

"Fuck, Sarah. You're so tight. You feel...." He groaned as he thrust. He shifted and she moaned as he hit a spot, a wonderful place that sent sparks flying through her body. "I can't..." His hand came down between them and he pinched her clit.

She screamed as he shoved her over the edge into ecstasy, her hips bucking against his and her inner walls clamping down on him.

"Oh, fuck!" He thrust twice more and shuddered, his back arching and collapsed on top of her.

She lay there, her hand trailing up and down his spine. His hot ragged breath against her neck.

"I'm squishing you." He lifted.

"No, not yet." She pressed him back down. She liked the feel of him on her, in her. Her bones were still liquid. She didn't feel his weight.

He relaxed, his body pushing her into the couch as he kissed her neck. "Tell me when I'm too heavy, but it'd better be soon or I'll fall asleep."

She skimmed her hands up his back as she kissed his ear. "Maybe, we should move to the bedroom."

He turned his face, kissing her. This one was soft and gentle with no agenda. Just a thank you.

CHAPTER 7: SARAH

Sarah moaned in her sleep as Adam's hand trailed down her stomach and lightly, too lightly, over her pussy. His fingers ran up and down the sides, caressing but never touching where she needed him to. She wiggled, trying to rub against his fingers but they were elusive.

"Please." She needed him to touch her, to fill her. She'd missed him so much.

"Open for me." His fingers delved into her moistness teasing as they played with her, circling her bud but that spot needed pressure, not light, teasing touches. His morning whiskers rubbed against her neck as he whispered in her ear. "Lift your leg."

She obeyed, tossing her leg over his and opening herself for his penetration. He was more than ready, his erection pressed against her butt and back.

"That's it baby." He kissed her neck and tore open a condom. He leaned away from her for a second and she scooted back, rubbing her ass against him. She didn't want to lose contact with him, not even for a moment. If she did, he'd disappear again.

"One minute, babe." There was humor in his voice. And then he was back, pressing against her. He grasped her hip. "Don't worry, Sarah, I'm going to fuck you hard just like you like it."

Her eyes flew open. This wasn't Adam. Adam was dead. This was someone else, a stranger. In one hard push, he was inside of her and she whimpered.

He stilled. "I'm sorry. Did I hurt you." His lips caressed her ear with his words.

She didn't want him. She wanted Adam, but Adam was gone and it wasn't Nick's fault. Still, she wanted to pull away. He didn't belong inside of her.

"Do you want me to stop?" He gave a small thrust as if his hips weren't listening to his words.

"No. I'm a little sore, that's all." If she told him to stop, there'd be questions and she wasn't going to talk to him about Adam. Not ever. They were fuck buddies, nothing else.

"Thank god." He kissed her ear, his tongue darting inside. "I probably would've cried." He thrust again. "I should've realized you'd be sore." He grinned against her neck. "This is the fourth time tonight, but I'll make it good for you. I'll go slow and gentle. You'll like that too. I promise."

She didn't want slow. She wanted this done. "It's okay."

He leaned over her and kissed her. "It's only okay if it's good for both of us." He deepened the kiss as his hands adjusted her hips and he thrust again, this time a little harder, a little deeper and a better, much better angle.

"Oh." That felt good. She pushed back against him.

"Found the spot, did I." He grinned as he buried his face in her neck and thrust in and out, again and again.

He kept hitting that one spot—the same place he'd found with his fingers—but it was so much better with his cock, hitting that bundle of nerves and sending jolts of pleasure zipping through her before joining forces and slamming back to her cunt. With every thrust, her body coiled tighter and tighter. She rocked against him, whimpers escaping her lips. Every time he hit that spot she came so close to climaxing. "Please...again...harder."

He did as she asked his breath coming in pants in her ear. Her hands grasped his on her hips, unwilling to let him go, let him change his position. He shoved into her harder and harder. His hand slipped out from under hers, stroking against her pussy, searching and then he pressed against her bud and held it down as he thrust into her.

The friction, the pressure was too much. She screamed her release, her back arching, causing his thrusts to go deeper. Her body thrummed and twitched as he continued to hit that spot over and over. She wriggled, trying to get away but his hand moved from her hip to her waist, holding her in place for his continued assault.

"Ni..." She couldn't form the word. She couldn't do anything but feel. She was going to die but he kept thrusting and the sensations shooting through her gathered and slammed her over the edge as another orgasm racked through her. Her muscles clasped his dick, squeezing.

"Fuck," he yelled as he shoved into her one more time, balls deep and grunted as his orgasm came.

Moments later he pulled out of her and rolled onto his back. "Shit, that was fantastic."

"Hmm." That was the best she could do. Words were still beyond her.

His hand trailed down her back and slipped for a moment between her butt cheeks. "I told you I was better than those other guys."

She stiffened. He wasn't better than Adam. This wasn't better than it'd been with Adam. It wasn't. This was just great sex. With Adam there'd been love, at least on her part. A wave of sadness threatened and she pushed it aside, focusing on her anger. He shouldn't even know about Adam. Her thoughts stumbled to a halt. He didn't know about Adam. He was talking about the other interview candidates.

He rolled her over and pulled her against his side. "I'm not usually one to say I told you so, but those clowns wouldn't have given you multiple orgasms like that."

Adam's memory was too close now and it didn't belong here in this bed. She didn't belong here in this bed. She wanted to leave. It was probably time, but she wasn't sure how to extricate herself at the moment. It seemed harsh to get up and leave after what they'd just done. She wrapped her arm around him, her hand caressing his chest, seeming unable to stop. He was warm and muscular and male. She'd missed men, but more importantly she'd missed Adam.

"You my dear are wearing me out." He yawned and kissed the top of her head. "I need a rest before the next round."

As soon as he was asleep she wriggled out from his hold and went into the bathroom. It was as gorgeous as the rest of the suite with a large, claw-footed tub and a separate shower. She wanted to shower, wipe Nick from her body but that sound might wake him so instead she turned on the faucet, sat on the toilet and cried. She shouldn't have done this. Adam wouldn't understand her being like this with a stranger. She needed to leave. She looked at her watch. She really needed to leave. It was almost four am. She stood and splashed water on her face. If Nick were awake she didn't want him to see that she'd been crying. He didn't deserve that.

She wrapped a towel around herself and slipped out of the bathroom, closing the door behind her. He was still asleep. She went into the living room and got dressed. She hesitated at the door. It seemed wrong to sneak away like this. She grabbed a pen and notepad from the desk but the pen froze over the paper. What should she write? Thanks seemed too vague. Thanks for the fuck was honest but she couldn't bring herself to write that. So, she quickly scrawled:

Nick,
  See you next week.
Sarah.

She slipped into the night, back to her life.

Book 2

Taking Control

CHAPTER 1: NICK

Nick was stretched out on the bed, his cock already hard, pressed into the mattress. His hand skimmed across the sheets, searching for Sarah. He was ready for another round. When he found nothing but sheets he leaned up. Her perfume lingered on the bedding making him even harder. Where the hell was she?

The bathroom door was closed, so he rolled over, waiting, the sheet tenting over his arousal. "Sarah, hurry up." It was rude. She may have only been in there a minute or two but he was horny. When she didn't answer, he got out of bed and knocked on the door. "Is everything okay?" Still nothing. No sound at all. Worry teased his mind. She might've fallen or something. "If you don't answer, I'm coming in." He waited another second or two and opened the door a crack, peering inside. It was empty.

She couldn't have left. She had to be in the living room or...the balcony. She wouldn't be able to hear him from the balcony. He hurried into the other room but it was empty too. Completely empty. No Sarah and no Sarah's clothes.

"Son-of-a-bitch." He scanned the room again. His brain unable to accept that she'd left. His eyes fell on a piece of paper on the table by the door. He strode over and picked it up. *Oh, she was going to pay for this.* He crumpled the note and tossed it across the room as he grabbed his cell phone from the table by the couch.

Ethan, his friend and owner of La Petite Mort Club, answered on the fourth ring. "Hello." His voice was rough with sleep.

"Call Sarah. I want to meet with her today. Today!"

"Jesus, Nick. Calm down. What happened?" Ethan was awake now.

"She left that's what happened?"

"She left? Before you—"

"No. We fucked." But not enough.

"Then—"

"She broke the contract."

"But she showed up and you had sex, right?"

"Yes." He knew where Ethan was heading but he refused to go there.

"Then, how did she break the contract?"

"She was supposed to spend the night." That sounded whiney to his own ears. "We had a deal."

"So, she left right after you had—"

"I don't know when she left. I was sleeping."

"Let me make sure I have this straight. She showed up. You had sex. You fell asleep and she left." Ethan sounded a little confused.

"No. She showed up and we fucked, several times and sometime later, when I was sleeping she snuck out."

"Snuck out?"

"Well, she didn't wake me."

"And you just realized this now, at five-thirteen a.m."

"Yeah."

"When was the last time you saw her?"

"I don't know what time it was. I woke. We had sex and I fell back asleep."

"So, she did spend the night."

"Not all of it." He'd planned on fucking her well into the morning, maybe even into the afternoon.

"Nick, stop being a baby. She didn't break the contract."

"She did and I want to renegotiate." He'd let her have her way far too much in the initial negotiations.

"You know that's only possible if the only other alternative is cancelling the contract. Are you ready to do that if she won't agree to new terms?"

She'd agree. He'd just given her multiple orgasms. She'd agree to anything he wanted. A twinge of doubt tickled his gut. She'd also left him in their warm bed and that wasn't something a woman who'd bend to his wishes would do.

"I hate to ask,"—Ethan paused—"but she did…enjoy the evening, right?"

"Of course, she did." He was insulted his friend had asked that. "The sex was great. Better than great. Fabulous."

"For her too."

"Yes, for her too." He wanted to throw the phone against the wall. "I'm not a novice."

"I know." Ethan hesitated. "Let me ask you again. Are you willing to risk five more nights of fabulous sex just to get her to agree to what...another couple of hours?"

"Yes." He'd risk it. She'd consent. She'd enjoyed herself as much as he had. Plus, he couldn't keep letting her do whatever she wanted.

Ethan sighed. "Are you sure? I'm only asking because...she has obligations that she won't bend on. Obligations I respect."

"What does that mean?"

"I encouraged you to come see her at the Viewing because I thought you'd be good for her. I like her, Nick. She's a good person who's had some rough times."

"But you won't tell me anything, including why she's leaving my bed in the middle of the night." Usually, he didn't care that Ethan never disclosed anything that was uncovered during the background checks, but he didn't like his friend knowing more about Sarah than he did.

"You know I can't and it's morning."

"Barely." He was usually up by now, but he'd wanted her here.

"One more time, are you—"

"I'm sure." He wasn't but he couldn't let Ethan know that. "And I want the meeting today."

"I can't guarantee I'll be able to reach her today."

"I don't care. Today or I cancel."

"Now, you're being a dick."

"Fine, but no later than tomorrow." He really didn't want to cancel and he wouldn't without seeing her. She may be able to resist him from a distance but she'd be as hot for him as he was for her once they were in the same room and that'd make her malleable to his will.

CHAPTER 2: SARAH

When Sarah walked into her house, Tank was waiting at the door. He almost vibrated with excitement as he barked and whined his greeting. She bent down, running her hands through his thick fur.

"It's okay, baby. Calm down." She should've never left him. He was panting and stressed. He pushed against her, sniffing and knocking her to the floor. At about one hundred pounds, Tank was big even for a Belgian Malinois. "I'm home now." She wrapped her arms around him and he rested his head against her chest for a second, seeming to sigh in relief and then he started sniffing her again. She needed to shower. Nick's scent had to be all over her.

"He did good tonight." Lisa was sitting on a pile of blankets on the floor next to Tank's bed. "He was a little nervous when you first left, but he settled down."

She gave the other woman a disbelieving look.

Tank's panting was just now slowing down.

"I swear." Lisa stood and started folding the blankets. "He was good until he heard your car."

"The guest bedroom not comfortable?"

"Tank didn't like it in there. He kept pacing. I didn't want him to get too upset, so we came out here."

"Oh. I'm sorry." She had to force the words past her lips. Lisa should be apologizing to her.

"No big deal. I've slept in more uncomfortable places than your floor."

"Right." She stood, trying to remember that Lisa was doing her a favor by staying here with Tank, but all she could think about was the past.

Lisa and Adam had met in Afghanistan. They'd fallen in love in Afghanistan. They'd had sex in Afghanistan and Adam had called her and broken her heart from Afghanistan. And then, he'd died there. She hated that place. She hated that word.

Lisa piled the blankets on the couch. "I should be going."

"Are you sure?" She wanted the other woman out of her house, but she'd been raised to be polite.

"Yeah. Tom and the kids will be getting up soon."

"Okay." Suddenly, she felt guilty and she hated it. Lisa was giving up time with her husband and kids to watch Tank. The other woman thought she was working late on a project that she couldn't do from home. Tank nudge her hand and dread settled in her stomach. "Are you sure he did okay? I can cancel the project." She really didn't want to do that. It'd be expensive and...she wanted to see Nick again.

"No." Lisa bent and stroked Tank's fur. "We had fun." Her eyes locked with Sarah's. "I swear, I'd tell you if he got too upset. I don't want anything to happen to him either, but he was good."

She took a deep breath. She may not like Lisa but Lisa loved Tank almost as much as she did. "Okay. Can you still watch him next Saturday?"

"Of course." Lisa kissed Tank's head. "I want to see my boy as much as I can before I deploy." She glanced up. "You're taking really good care of him. Thank you."

She nodded, her throat tight. "I try."

"Well, you're doing great." Lisa stroked his fur. "I know it's not easy. He was a real wreck when Adam died." She buried her face in Tank's neck. "I thought we were going to lose him too. You saved his life." She stood, tears in her eyes. "Thank you again for taking him and for letting me visit him all these years." She stared at Tank. "I know it wasn't easy for you."

"No, it wasn't, but…it was the best thing for Tank." She scratched his ear, taking a deep breath. Lisa was doing her a favor and it was time, past time, for this. "I never thanked you for contacting me about him. I think he saved my life too." She smiled at the other woman. It was the first genuine smile she'd ever given Lisa.

"Oh." Surprise and gratitude sparkled in Lisa's eyes. "I'll see you next Saturday."

"You can sleep on the couch." It wasn't much of a concession but it was something.

"Nah. I tried that. Tank was too anxious. He was better with me on the floor." Lisa opened the door and hesitated. "Have you tried taking him to one of your doctors? You know the ones that work with the PTSD dogs."

It was none of Lisa's business. Tank was her responsibility, but she kept her temper in check. "It's hard. He panics if we go outside, except in the back yard. There's too much stimulation for him."

"Oh." Lisa opened her mouth as if to say something, paused and then said, "I should go."

"Goodnight and thank you." She shut the door. She didn't want a lecture about what was best for Tank from Lisa. It was bad enough she got one regularly from her mother and sister.

She went into her bedroom, pulling off her clothes as she walked. Taking care of Tank was her job and of course, she'd tried everything to help him. She knew what she was doing. Her business specialized in treating emotionally injured animals, mainly dogs. She dealt a lot with military dogs and sometimes, PTSD couldn't be fixed. Like humans, sometimes the mental anguish the animals suffered wasn't repairable. Then, like with Tank, they did whatever they could to make the animal comfortable for the rest of his or her life.

She turned on the water and stepped into the shower, washing away Nick's scent. Too bad the memories of his touch weren't as easy to remove. Her body refused to forget how he'd made her feel—desirable, sexy, hot and needy. A throbbing started between her legs. She pushed all thoughts of Nick and last night from her head. She was home. Nick didn't belong here.

She turned off the shower and got ready for bed. She crawled under her covers and grabbed her phone to set her alarm. She'd missed a call. She didn't recognize the number. She logged into voice mail as Tank hopped on the bed and snuggled up against her side. She stroked his fur and her hand froze as she heard Ethan's message. Nick wanted to meet, to renegotiate or he was cancelling their contract.

CHAPTER 3: SARAH

Sarah followed Ethan down the hallway. She had no idea what she'd done to upset Nick enough to cancel their arrangement. She'd thought they'd both had a good time, proving once again she had no idea what men wanted.

"I'll let you two talk. Hopefully, you can work this out." Ethan stopped in front of a closed door.

She nodded, her words getting caught in her throat. What was it about her that made men walk away without a second thought?

"Just hear him out." Ethan opened the door and stepped aside.

Nick was sitting at the table, his back to her. It wasn't a good sign that he didn't even turn as she came inside. The door closed behind her but she stayed where she was. Her heart trying to pound its way up her chest and out her mouth. He wore business clothes today—black slacks and a white shirt that stretched over his broad shoulders. She remembered how his skin felt, hot and firm and his short black hair, so thick and soft. She wanted to run her fingers over his shoulders and into his hair, but that'd be a mistake today.

"Are you going to stand there staring at me or are you going to take a seat so we can get this settled?" Other than taking a drink from his glass of scotch, he didn't move.

Another glass was on the table across from him. Probably, Crown for her but she wasn't drinking tonight. She should because even though part of her regretted this sexual arrangement, another part of her didn't want it to end. It'd been so good to be with a man and she wasn't going through the club's process again. That meant, she was back to her lonely life. No. She wasn't lonely. She had her work and Tank. She didn't need anyone else, to hell with Nick.

She strode forward and sat at the table, looking directly at him even though it hurt. She'd seen that handsome face laugh and be kind and in the moment of ecstasy. It was hard to see the anger in his eyes. "I'm not sure what we have to work out."

"Really? You don't think there's anything about the other night we should discuss?"

"I...I said I was sorry about being nervous at first, but I thought we got through that."

"This isn't about you being nervous. That was fine. It ended up...very good."

She flushed. She'd enjoyed their game too and had looked forward to more.

"Nothing else comes to mind?"

She shook her head. The rest of the night had been excellent, except when she'd confused him for Adam and had almost cried, but there was no way he knew anything about that.

He leaned forward. "You don't feel even the littlest bit of remorse for sneaking out in the middle of the night before you'd satisfied the terms of our contract?"

"This is because I left?"

"Yes." He leaned back, seeming pleased with himself. "You broke our deal."

"I did no such thing. I agreed to spend the night. I did."

"You did not." His voice was hard and his dark eyes snapped with anger.

"I arrived on Saturday and left on Sunday. Later than I should have, just so you know." This was absurd. He was being absurd.

"Later?" He almost stood. "You left before dawn. What time were you planning on leaving, twelve-o-one?"

"No. I wanted to leave, needed to leave, by three. I didn't leave until four. I was..." She'd almost said late but that'd bring too many questions.

"Three? No." He shook his head. "That's not going to work."

"You should've thought of that when we were signing the contract." She stood. There was no reason for her to be here.

"Sit down."

She almost sat at the command, but she stopped herself. She wasn't his employee or his slave. "I have to go."

"That seems to be a habit. One you need to break."

"Too bad." She headed for the door. The man had a lot of nerve making her come down here after they'd agreed...

"Then, I'm cancelling the contract."

She spun around. "On what grounds?"

He turned. "I don't need grounds. If I'm unhappy with the arrangement and I am, I can cancel after the first appointment."

A heaviness settled in her stomach. He wasn't kidding. She walked back to the table and sat. She hated cowing to his wishes but she wanted to be with him again. After these six nights, she'd go back to being alone, but she really wanted this time. "I...I wish you wouldn't."

Her confession seemed to erase some of his anger. "I don't want to," he said softly.

"Then don't."

"I need you to stay through the night. Into the morning. Late morning."

"I...I can't." She reached across the table and touched his hand. It was a fleeting gesture but it sent a spark zinging through her body and settling between her legs. She wanted him right now.

"Why?" His voice was hard again.

"I...I can't explain. It's personal."

"Fuck personal. Tell me or we end this."

She shook her head. She couldn't explain Tank. That'd bring up Adam and he didn't have any place in a relationship like this one. "I'm sorry. I can't." She fought the tears. She wouldn't cry in front of him. She wouldn't. "I...you should know that if I could, I'd stay later, but I really can't."

He tossed back the rest of his drink, watching her for several minutes. "You aren't going home to a husband or lover. Ethan would've had that in the dossier."

"There's no one."

"Then why do you have to leave at three a.m.?"

She remained silent. She'd answered him the best she could.

"Do you have a kid?"

She shook her head. It was like a punch to the gut. No, she didn't have a child. The baby had died too. Adam's baby. Her baby.

"Then I don't understand."

"I'm sorry." She couldn't do this. The ghosts of Adam and their child were here now, haunting her memory. She stood. "I'm sorry. Truly, I am." She headed to the door. She'd remember the look on his face for the rest of her life. Shock, disbelief and humor all mixed as if she were joking, had to be joking. She wished she were.

"Wait." He almost shouted.

She stopped her hand on the doorknob.

"I want another night."

"We've already gone over this. I can't."

"You're here now. You made time today."

"Barely." She looked at her watch. "And I can't stay long." As it was, she'd had to get her sister to come by and sit with Tank. He liked Maisie and her son but after a couple of hours he started to stress. He was almost ten and his heart wasn't good. She'd die if something happened to him because she was out having sex.

"I don't need long." He walked over to her. "An

hour at the most."

She could manage an hour. Her heart picked up its pace. Desire filled his eyes and she squeezed her thighs together.

"I...I...can't find the time often."

"Three times a week."

He was so close now she could feel the heat from his body and her nipples hardened. It was like he had a sixth sense about sex because his eyes dropped to her chest.

"Once every other week. I may be able to figure out—"

"Once a week." He ran his thumb over her breast, playing with her nipple through her blouse.

"Okay." She shouldn't have agreed without talking to Maisie, but she'd figure something out if her sister refused. "I'm not sure which day though."

"That's fine. Let me know on Saturday or let Ethan know."

She nodded, her breathing becoming labored.

"I want to meet earlier on Saturday too." He leaned down and kissed her neck.

She shivered and tipped her head to the side, giving his talented lips better access. "I can be there by six." When they'd first discussed it, Lisa had said she could arrive by five.

"Can you make it earlier?" His lips teased her ear and his tongue darted inside.

"No. Sorry." She grasped his shirt, feeling his heat and his muscles.

"Too bad. Nine hours won't be nearly enough." His hand grabbed her breast, squeezing and she whimpered.

"Same place," she asked.

"Saturday and next week, yes." He moved closer, his other hand pulling her against him, into his arousal. She wriggled her hips, rubbing against him and he inhaled sharply.

"What about this week?" She was pretty sure she knew the answer.

He picked her up, his hands under her ass and carried her across the room.

"Right here. Right now." He put her down and moved behind her, pushing her top half onto the table.

"Here?" She squeaked but her arousal hitched into overdrive. "Anyone can walk in." Like that girl had done before.

He leaned over and whispered in her ear. "I know." He rubbed his erection against her ass and then straightened.

"Lock the..." Her words died as his hands trailed up the outside of her legs pulling her skirt with them.

"Did you wear these for me?" He cupped her ass.

She'd started to say no, that she always wore sexy underwear but his thumbs dipped between her cheeks skimming downward and the lie disappeared. "Yes."

"Thank you." He bent, and kissed her ass, first one cheek and then the other, as his fingers drifted along the sides of her pussy. "You're already soaked."

She arched her back, pushing herself toward him. She needed him to touch her, now, but his fingers stayed inches away from where she wanted them, needed them. She shifted again and he nipped her butt.

"Hey!"

He licked where he'd bitten her—his tongue hot and wet. She moaned, reaching back to touch him. He yanked the black lace panties down her legs and she kicked them away. She didn't want anything between them. He unzipped his pants as he shoved her legs apart and stepped between them. His dick, hot and hard, pushed against her ass before finding its way between her thighs. She arched her back, trying to get closer to him, to what she wanted and he pushed her legs even farther apart, as he pulled her away from the table a few inches. He thrust, his cock stroking along her cunt and she moaned. He was so hot and so hard.

"Again. Please. Nick."

He rocked against her as his hand wrapped into her hair, pulling back her head. "I'm going to fuck you now. Hard and fast." He rubbed his cock against her clit. "If someone comes in,"—he panted in her ear—"they're going to see a show because I'm not going to stop."

She glanced at the door. People did shows at this club but that wasn't her thing. "Please, lock the door."

"No." He nipped her ear. "You'd better do exactly as I say, or I'm going to call for a maid."

"Don't." She tried to get up. She'd lock the door herself, but his weight kept her from moving.

"Hold still." His other hand moved to her pussy and he stroked her as he rubbed his dick through her wetness. "No matter what you feel...do...not...move." With each word, his finger tapped her little bud, sending shockwaves of desire through her.

"Please." Her body was tensing. She was so close. She shifted against his hand.

"Do that again and I swear I'll get everyone within hearing distance in her."

She froze, but she couldn't stop the trembling as he continued to stroke her. His fingers and his dick working in tandem to keep the sensations zipping through her body. She struggled not to move, not to come because if she came, there was no stopping her body from moving.

"That's a good girl." His breathing was ragged. He was close too and that meant this exquisite torture was almost over.

He let go of her hair and stepped back. "Don't move."

She lay there, half resting on the table with her legs spread wide. The idea of him staring at her like this made wetness run down her thighs and she rubbed against the table.

"I saw that," he said.

"Please, Nick."

"Please Nick, what?" His hand caressed her ass. "Don't call everyone in here or please Nick, fuck me?"

"Please Nick, fuck me." Right now, all she wanted was him inside of her.

There was the tearing of a condom wrapper and then he was back. His hand tangled in her hair again and she winced as he pulled her head backward but then his lips found her neck and he sucked as he shoved inside of her, filling her. She moaned – partially from the intrusion, she was still sore from the other night, but mostly because this was exactly what she'd wanted, needed.

He rocked into her and she pushed back against him, meeting him thrust for thrust. His hands moved to her hips, adjusting her position and she almost screamed as he found a rhythm and position that hit all the right spots inside of her while his pressure and motion caused her clit to rub against the table.

"Oh, yes. There. Please."

He thrust. "Here." He shifted and thrust again. "Or here."

"Oh, God! There. Harder."

"Or here wins." He slammed into her over and over.

"Don't stop. Please." She no longer cared where they were. She didn't care if a hundred people walked in. She still wouldn't want him to stop.

He grabbed her hair again and he pulled her back as he leaned down. "Come for me, baby." He kept pushing into her. His cock seeming to get longer and harder with each thrust.

His words pushed her over the edge and she convulsed, her body bucking and her pussy clamping down on his dick, trying to milk it for its seed.

He thrust into her another couple of times and groaned as he came, collapsing on top of her. "Fuck."

"I think we covered that." She liked the feel of his strong body wrapped around her, inside of her. She didn't want to move. Ever.

He kissed her ear as he stood. "That we did."

CHAPTER 4: NICK

At the first knock, Nick opened the door. Just the thought of Sarah had made him hard. His nostrils flared when he saw her. Everything but lust left his brain and body.

She had her hair pulled up in an elegant chignon and she wore a sexy black dress that hugged her curves. She looked sophisticated, untouchable and he wanted her on her knees sucking his cock. He frowned slightly as his gaze landed on her shoes—flats again. He stepped aside. He'd make her take them off. Bare feet were sexy.

"Hi," she said as she slipped past him.

He inhaled sharply as her breast brushed against his arm. That'd been on purpose. He'd given her plenty of room. Someone wanted to tease. He was more than up for that. He closed the door, leaning against it. "Take off your clothes."

She turned and smiled at him. "No. You called the

shots the last time at the club. Tonight, I'm in charge."

"Okay. I'll play." He grinned. He enjoyed sex games and this one promised to be interesting.

She pointed to the couch. "Sit your sexy ass down."

"Yes, ma'am." He chuckled as he moved to the couch and sat.

She went to the liquor cabinet and made them both a drink. Her hand shook as she gulped down a large swallow of hers.

"You haven't ever done this, have you?" he asked.

She carried the drinks over and handed him his. "That obvious, huh?"

"A little."

"Oh." She seemed to deflate and it tugged at his heart.

"It's okay. Everything's new for all of us at some point." He took a sip of his drink and stretched his arm along the back of the couch. "Do what you like, what makes you feel good." His gazed skimmed over her chest and rested on the juncture between her legs. "What makes you wet." She'd better hurry or he'd take over. His dick was already pressing uncomfortably against his zipper.

"I'll try but...if you don't like something—"

"I'll like anything you do." His eyes met hers. "And if for some reason I don't, I'll let you know. Just like you're to let me know if I do anything you don't like. Honesty between us - always."

She smiled shyly. "Okay." She tossed back the rest of her drink and set the glass on the coffee table. "I bought these for you." She stepped out of her flats and took some sexy-as-hell high heels out of her bag. She glanced at him as she turned sideways and lifted her left leg.

It was the one closest to him and her position made her dress slide toward her hips, giving him a good view of her long leg. The dark green garter belt, holding up the sheer stockings, caused his dick to harden even more. He tugged on his pants. If she weren't careful, her little game was going to end soon. She put that foot down and replaced it with the other one. He almost groaned. Her inner thigh was begging for him to kiss it. He leaned forward, his hand travelling up her left leg and his mouth aiming for her right. It'd been too long since he'd tasted her and he was going to fix that right now.

She slapped his hand and shoved his shoulder, pushing him toward the couch. "Did I say you could touch?"

"What?" He frowned at her. She had to be kidding.

"Don't touch, unless I tell you to." She finished buckling the shoe and moved her foot to the floor. "Or do I have to tie you up?"

His eyes locked with hers as desire slammed through him. He almost grabbed her and fucked her right there, but the mischievousness in her eyes halted him. She was having fun. He shifted to ease the pressure in his pants. He could handle a little more. "No ma'am. I'll behave."

"Good." She stepped closer and gave his foot a little kick.

He spread his legs. She moved between them and bent, displaying her breasts. His mouth watered and his hands itched to touch them. Her fingers lifted his chin so he was forced to look in her eyes. She smiled and her soft lips pressed against his. He grasped the couch, holding on tight because he wanted to shove his hands in her hair, removing her chignon and letting her hair hang down over her shoulders. Her tongue skimmed across his lips and he forced himself to remain passive.

"You can kiss me back," she said, a slight pout in her tone.

"I wasn't sure."

"Well, you can." She kissed him again and this time he didn't hold back.

He leaned forward, his hands cupping her face and positioning her for the best access. His tongue thrust into her mouth, meeting hers and tangling together, reminding her of exactly what he wanted to do to her body, would do to her body. A few moments later when her hands pushed his arms down and she pulled back, he almost snarled. He hadn't been done kissing her yet, not by a long shot.

She stepped back. "Close your legs."

He tossed back the rest of his drink, anything to cool his blood, and did as she commanded. She moved forward, hands on his shoulders as she straddled his lap. His dick leaped and his hips came up, thrusting his cock against her.

"Oh," she moaned as she pushed down against him and rocked. "You...weren't supposed to do that."

His hands trailed up her legs, pushing her dress out of his way as his fingers brushed against her pussy. She was soaked and he needed to get out of his pants and into her.

"Don't touch." She slapped him again.

His jaw clenched. This was getting old.

"You agreed. I'm in charge tonight."

"For now."

"For tonight."

His eyes met hers. There was no way she was
staying in charge all night but there was no reason to argue.
He'd hold out as long as he could, but he hadn't had sex
since their renegotiation and he was about ready to blow.
He nodded and she smiled, making his heart skip a beat.
He'd do his best to let her finish her game.

Her hands moved from his shoulders down his
chest, exploring. As her fingers skimmed over his
abdomen he tipped back his head, his hands clenched at his
sides. If she didn't touch him soon, he'd beg. He never
begged but tonight he would. He needed to feel her hands
on him that badly. Her fingers dipped into his pants but all
she did was tug his shirt free.

"Tease," he said.

She kissed his neck, licking and sucking. He
moaned and his hands skimmed down her back for one
quick trip and then moved back to the couch, grasping the
cloth.

"Raise your arms," she whispered against his ear.

If she stuck her tongue in his ear, it was over.
Game time was done.

"Raise your arms," she repeated. "Or do you want
me to stand up." She rubbed against him for emphasis, like
he didn't know what he'd be losing.

He lifted his arms and she pulled his shirt up and
over his head.

"Good boy."

He started to argue that he wasn't a boy but then her

hands were exploring and he forgot about everything but her cool hands on his hot flesh, her nails scraping along his skin followed by her lips and tongue. She was touching him everywhere except where he needed it most.

He thrust up, against her. "Unzip my pants."

"Not yet." She kissed him hard on the lips.

He grabbed her arms, holding her in place but as soon as she stopped kissing him, he let go. This was her game, her rules and for her he could hold out a little longer. She stood and he reached for her, his instincts screaming to tear her underwear off and bring her back to his lap, but he stopped before he touched her.

"Good boy." Her eyes sparkled at him.

"I'm not a boy or a damn dog. Get back over here." He was about done with this. If he didn't get out of his pants soon his dick was going to have zipper prints permanently embedded in it.

"Not yet." She took a step back and her hands went to her zipper.

His breath froze in his chest. It was time. There was no way he'd be able to keep from touching her, fucking her once she was naked.

CHAPTER 5: SARAH

Sarah's fingers fumbled with the zipper. She was soaking wet and he felt so good pushing against her but she wanted to delay this a little longer. She was having fun torturing him. She slid the zipper down and shimmied out of the dress. His eyes raked over her slowly and his face hardened. She didn't have much more time before he snapped.

"Give me your foot?"

"What?" He shook his head. "Never mind. Which one?"

"Doesn't matter."

He raised his leg and she turned around and stepped over his knee, keeping one foot on each side. She bent at the waist. Her face heated as she began to untie his shoe. He had a perfect view of her ass. The black and green thong wasn't going to hide much. His ragged breathing filled the room. She pulled off his shoe and sock.

"You can lower your leg now."

He did.

"Give me the other one."

He obeyed and she moved to stand over this leg like the last one, bending again to remove his shoe. Her knees almost buckled as his fingers skimmed over her ass and his hot breath seeped into the crease as both his hands grasped onto her hips.

"No touching." The words came out as a pant.

"I'm helping. I know you're unsteady in those shoes."

"Okay." She was unsteady but more importantly she didn't want him to let go.

His thumbs drew circles on her cheeks as she pulled off his shoe and sock. When his open-mouth kiss landed on her ass and his tongue delved into the crease she tightened her grasp on his foot, anything to keep from falling face first into the coffee table.

"Stop that." He sat up, a burst of laughter coming from him.

She glanced at him, over her shoulder. "You're ticklish." That was the last thing she'd expected.

"I am not." He grabbed her hips again, pulling her toward him, but she had a weapon now.

She tapped her fingers along the sole of his foot and his leg twitched, trying to free his foot from her, as he started laughing.

"Stop it."

"Oh, no." She did it again and his arm wrapped around her waist, hauling her down to the couch and against his chest. "That's cheating," she said as she struggled to free herself.

"And tickling me isn't." His fingers poked along her side. "I can tickle you too."

"Stop," she laughed as his fingers found the spot. She squirmed and then stilled as her butt rubbed against his erection.

His hands moved to her thighs, spreading them apart.

"Thanks for the heels. They're hot as hell." His fingers drifted toward her pussy, but stopped only inches away. "Can I touch?" He nipped her ear.

Oh, she wanted to say "yes" but then her time in control would be over. "No."

His sharp intake of breath almost made her laugh. He hadn't expected that. His fingers skimmed over her underwear.

"Are you sure? You're soaking wet." His words caressed her ear as he stroked her pussy. "Are you positive you want me to stop?"

She didn't. She did. "Yes. Stop." She tugged on his wrist until he moved his hand. Part of her wanted to cry at the loss, but this was her night. She turned so she was once again straddling him. Her eyes locked with his as she lowered herself against him and rubbed right where she'd wanted him to touch. She whimpered. He felt so good, so right.

"Unzip me, please."

She kissed his neck as she rocked against him. "Not yet." She leaned back, keeping her pussy pressed against his cock as she reached around her back.

His dark eyes zeroed in on her breasts as she

unhooked her bra. She held it in front of her for a second or so, watching his face as it hardened even more. He licked his lips, a quick little lick but it was like he'd touched her with his tongue. She dropped her bra and his eyes darkened.

She leaned forward, her hand trailing down his chest to his pants. His hands moved to her waist and upward, cupping her breasts.

"Did I tell you that you could touch me?"

"I'm not." He squeezed and his fingers pinched her nipple.

She moaned and unbuttoned his pants. "Liar."

She dipped her fingers under his waistband feeling the top of his penis. It was hot and hard and ready for her. She carefully unzipped his pants and scooted back and stood. Her legs shook with desire and his hands grabbed her hips steadying her. She pulled her underwear down and stepped out of them. She put her foot on his thigh. "Take off my shoe."

"Leave them on." He lifted her foot and kissed her toes, his eyes meeting hers. "And the stockings. Please."

"Okay." She'd do whatever he wanted when he looked at her like that—all hot desire and need. She glanced down at his crotch where his penis jutted proudly from his lap. "Your pants."

"Won't get in the way." He pulled a condom from his back pocket and lifted slightly, shoving his pants down his hips. He grabbed her hand, tugging her toward him.

She knelt over his thighs.

"Touch me," his words were a plea.

She wrapped her hands around his thick shaft,

95

reveling in the velvety hardness of him. She licked her lips and bent toward him. She wanted to taste him.

He grabbed her chin, stopping her. "Later. I'll never last this time and I want to be inside you when I come." He tore open a condom and slid it down his dick. "Now, Sarah."

His patience was gone. This was the most control she could still have. If she disobeyed, he'd do what he wanted. She wrapped her hands around him again and lowered herself, rubbing his cock along her slit and moaning as his heat and hardness pressed against her clit. She lifted and did it again and again. She was so close to coming, just another couple of times.

"Fuck, Sarah. Enough with the games."

He jerked her forward, thrusting his hips upward. She gasped as he shoved into her, all the way, stretching her, filling her. Her body already coiled tight exploded and she rocked against him as she came.

"Shit. You feel so good." He thrust into her again and again as she clamped down around him.

She wrapped her arms around his neck, her breasts smashed against his chest as she bucked with her release. He thrust one more time, groaning into her neck as he came.

Several moments later, he muttered against her neck, "I'm buying this couch when our time is up. I fucking love this couch."

She laughed, holding him tighter against her.

Book 3

School Fantasy

CHAPTER 1: NICK

Nick checked his watch as Ethan sat down at the table. "You're late." He pulled a manila envelope from his briefcase and handed it to his friend. "Give this to Sarah." He'd let her take control last weekend, but this Saturday was his turn.

Monica, the waitress, hurried over. "Hi Ethan. Haven't seen you around in a while."

"I'll have the burger, medium with salad on the side." Ethan barely looked at the girl and she wasn't happy about it.

"I'll have the pepper steak, fries on the side and a refill." He held out his almost empty glass of iced tea.

"Yeah. Sure." She gave Ethan another seductive look. "And what would you like...to drink?"

It used to bother him that Ethan seemed to cast a spell over every woman he met but he'd outgrown that years ago. He could have her later if he wanted. She'd be in Ethan's employ before long.

"Iced tea, no sugar." When she continued to stand there, Ethan looked up at her. "Did you need something else?"

"No." She huffed and strode away.

"Hasn't taken the bait yet, huh?" he asked.

"Almost." Ethan stared at the waitress until she looked his way and then he quickly averted his eyes. "I think today will do it."

Ethan was an expert at attracting and catching women. Once he found a girl he wanted to recruit—usually waitresses, bartenders, etc.—he'd hang out where she worked for months, flirting with her. Eventually, he'd give her his card and offer to show her around the place. Some women were immediately intrigued by the sex club. They'd show up, he'd take them on a tour, seduce them and offer them a job. Others, like Monica, took more time.

Monica returned with their drinks and glanced around.

"Is there something else?" Ethan's gaze roamed up her body to her face.

Her breathing increased, making her breasts press against her shirt. "Yeah." She glanced around again. "I was wondering if you still wanted to…"

"Wanted to what, Monica?"

She took a deep breath. "Show me around your club." A hint of a blush crept into her cheeks.

Ethan smiled as he took her hand. "I'd love nothing

more." His fingers caressed her skin. "Give me your address and I'll send a car for you. Be ready at ten." He looked up at her as he kissed her palm. "Expect to be out late."

"What should I wear? I've never been to a place like that." She scribbled on her order pad and handed the paper to him.

"Something sexy is best, but you can wear anything. People come in shorts, jeans, business attire, lingerie and everything in between." Ethan kissed her hand again and by her shiver, he'd used his tongue, before letting her go. "I'll see you tonight."

She smiled and left.

"You want to join us?" Ethan took a drink.

"How do you know she'd even be willing to do both of us? Usually, you wait until you've fucked them a few times before you initiate a ménage." He and Ethan had participated in threesomes many times over the years. It was one of the ways Ethan broke his new girls into the club scene.

"She's interested." Ethan's eyes wandered to Monica again. "She's ready to experiment, break out of her shell." He looked back at Nick. "I've been doing this a long time. I can tell. She'll be nervous but willing."

He had no doubt that Ethan was right. The man had a sixth sense about these things. "Thanks, but I'm in a contract, remember?"

"One that doesn't obligate you to be celibate on your off nights."

"I know but I want to convince Sarah to forego condoms." He really wanted to feel her without the rubber between them. Feel her heat and her muscles clamping down on his bare cock. He needed to stop thinking about that or he'd cause a scene when he left. His dick was already rising for action.

"We'll use them with Monica so you'll be safe."

"But I'll have to tell Sarah and…there's no way she'll agree if she knows I've been with someone else. Even protected."

Ethan studied him. "Telling her isn't required. She knows what's in the contract."

"I know that." Great. Now, Ethan would think there was more to his relationship with Sarah than sex. "But, thanks to you, I've learned honesty in these situations is best."

"I agree, but I hadn't realized you believed that too." Ethan continued to watch him closely. "The sex is better if you're both honest."

The sex couldn't get any better between him and Sarah, but it could go bad and he'd do anything he had to in order to keep that from happening. "Exactly. And since I really want to eliminate condoms, a night with your new protégé won't work."

"Are you sure?" Ethan looked at the waitress. "She's young, beautiful and this will be her first foray into something other than typical sex."

He studied Monica. She was beautiful, with long, straight, black hair and an olive complexion, but he wasn't in the mood. "Yeah, I'm sure."

"I guess I'll ask Patrick." Ethan smiled at Monica as she brought their lunches to the table.

"Enjoy." Her eyes devoured Ethan.

"Oh, we will, especially tonight."

"I have no doubt." Her eyes ran over Ethan's frame.

"I was thinking about inviting Nick"—he nodded at his friend—"to join us."

He sent Ethan a glare but his friend only had eyes for the waitress.

Monica glanced at Nick, her eyes roaming over him. "I...I'm not sure."

"I think you are." Ethan took her hand. "Nick's a good guy. Very good."

She flushed.

"You don't have to do anything you don't want to." Ethan kissed her hand again. "You'll never have to do anything you don't want to. Not with me. Not at my club."

"Promise?"

"Absolutely."

Her gaze darted to Nick. "Then okay."

"Fabulous." Ethan smiled and let go of her hand.

Another customer waved at her. "I've got to go." She left.

"Why'd you do that. I told you I wasn't interested." Sometimes Ethan pushed too hard, expecting everyone to bow to his will, but he wouldn't. Not this time.

"Fine. Sleep alone dreaming of Sarah."

"I'm not dreaming of Sarah." He was. Every night. "I have a lot of work to do. You'll be working. I won't."

"Should've started a different business." Ethan took a bite of his burger.

"The area won't support another high-end sex club and I'm not moving." Plus, he liked what he did. He enjoyed helping start-ups navigate the business world and get their brand noticed.

"You could've partnered with me."

"That would've never worked. You like to have your own way and so do I." They'd been friends for years. Ethan had been one of his first customers and had tried to get him to buy into La Petite Mort Club, but he'd refused, knowing it'd ruin their friendship and probably both businesses.

Ethan shrugged. "Suit yourself."

"What are you going to tell her when Patrick is there instead of me."

"She won't care."

"Ouch." He ate a bite of his sandwich, not really caring that Monica would substituted him for Patrick without a second thought. Sarah wouldn't and that was all that mattered at the moment. "I'll never understand how you know this about women." He wasn't a novice but Ethan was...something else.

"You over think it. Women have most men fooled into thinking they're unique, complex creatures, but they're not. Take Monica. She was attracted to me by my looks and money. Like men are attracted to women by their looks and sometimes money. I flirted with her and because she's beautiful, she thought she held the cards. When she refused my offer to visit the club, she was so sure I'd bend to her wishes." Ethan smiled. "I didn't. Instead, I ignored her." He glanced at the waitress. "Like most beautiful women, she isn't used to being ignored and she doesn't like it. Not at all. She'll make a good domme."

Nick shook his head. "I don't know if I admire you

or pity you."

Ethan's eyes hardened. "Both would ruin our friendship."

"Oh, don't get pissed off." He should've never said pity. Ethan had grown up poorer than poor and despised any kind of pity or charity. "You know you're like a brother to me."

Ethan grunted and finished his burger before starting on his salad. "Well brother, I guess I should tell you the bad news." He picked up the envelope Nick had given him.

"If Sarah cancelled..." He'd kill her. No, he'd drag her address out of Ethan and go to her house. She could tell him to his face...

"Calm down." Ethan opened his satchel, put Nick's envelope inside and pulled out a different one. He slid it across the table. "Your...plans will have to wait for the following Saturday."

"What?" He snatched the envelope. "Sarah gave you..." Sure, she'd enjoyed being in control but to write out her fantasy and hand it over to Ethan...He was shocked. Aroused but shocked.

"Yep." Ethan grinned. "I told you she was special."

His fingers itched to open the envelope and immerse himself in Sarah's fantasy. Would she want to be dominant this weekend? Submissive? He had no idea. She'd been both on different occasions.

"I think this is the first time one of your...partners beat you to this point in the game."

He grunted an agreement as he forced himself to put

the envelope in his briefcase. He needed to get back to his office, shut the door and look over these papers.

"Go. Read. I got this." Ethan pulled out his wallet.

CHAPTER 2: NICK

Nick paced in the hotel living room while Sarah got ready—whatever that meant—in the bedroom. According to her instructions, he'd had this room rearranged. He frowned at the couch, his favorite piece of furniture ever, as it sat abandoned in the corner. In its place was a desk with two chairs, one behind it and one in front. It had a few books, papers, pens and a laptop on it.

He loved the couch but the desk might be fun too. He could sit her on top or bend her over it while he fucked her from behind. He tugged on the front of his dress slacks, his thoughts not helping his already partially aroused state. He wasn't sure how her fantasy of the naughty professor would play out, but it didn't matter. Sarah was here so he was hard. It was like his dick remembered how fucking good she felt and it was eager to get back inside of her.

There was a light knock on the door that separated

the bedroom from the living room.

He moved behind the desk and sat, staring at the laptop. "Yes."

The door opened and his dick twitched in his pants as Sarah stepped out of the bedroom dressed in a Catholic school girl's uniform, complete with plaid skirt and white shirt buttoned to the throat. Her long hair was pulled back in a pony-tail. She looked about sixteen. He closed his eyes for a moment, thanking God she wasn't.

"Professor, may I speak with you about the grade on my last paper." She kept looking down at her feet, as if shy.

"My office hours are on the door." Even though he wanted to grab her and run his hands up under her little uniform, he wasn't going to make this easy for her.

Her eyes widened a bit in surprise. In her papers, she'd summarized how the scene was to work but the actions and dialogue were open for interpretation by the participants, as all good fantasies should be, which meant he'd make her work for it. A professor wouldn't jump any girl who walked into his office. A naughty professor had to be very careful.

"Oh." She bit her lip.

He held back a groan. He wanted to do that.

"Lucy said..." She grabbed her ponytail and twirled a strand of hair around her fingers.

"Lucy said what?" According to his notes, Lucy was the professor's procurer.

"Well, ah...she said I shouldn't come during your regular office hours. Not if I wanted...wanted you to maybe give me some extra work to improve my grade."

She moved another step into the room.

"And why would I do that?" A man who was preying on his students had to be sure they were willing.

"I...I...I don't know. I was upset about my grade and Lucy said that maybe...maybe you'd help me out because it was my birthday—"

"Happy birthday. How old?" He prayed she was of age because he didn't want to play the pedophile. It was bad enough playing the pervert.

"Eighteen."

He fought a grin. He'd have to thank Sarah later for that gift. "What exactly did Lucy tell you?"

"She said I should come and see you and tell you she'd sent me." She bowed her head, hiding the tears that welled in her eyes. "I really can't have a D. I can't." Her lips trembled and she turned to leave. "I'm sorry I bothered you."

"Wait." He stood, pulling his cardigan—which he'd had to purchase for this fantasy—over the bulge in his pants.

She stopped, turning around, hope in her gorgeous green eyes.

He felt like a cad. He wasn't sure this fantasy was for him, but he'd play along. He wasn't actually a pervert since this girl... "What's your name?"

"Mary."

"Of course, it is." He smiled to take the sting from his words. The bleeding, bloody, virgin Mary. "Close the door and have a seat."

He pulled out the chair in front of the desk and as soon as she sat he moved behind his desk and put on his best professor's face.

"So Mary, how important is getting a good grade in English to you?" He tried to keep his eyes on her face but he really wanted to know what she was wearing under that uniform. The white shirt wasn't thin but it wasn't thick enough to completely hide her bra. It looked like the innocent, plain white variety and he must be getting into this fantasy, because the thought of her in nothing but plain, white cotton bra and panties was making his dick swell uncomfortably. Of course, she could be wearing a thong— a present waiting to be unwrapped

"It means everything to me. My parents can't afford to pay for college. I...I have to get a scholarship. I'll die if I have to stay here."

"Now Mary, you won't die."

"No." Her lower lip came out in a pout and he wanted to run his tongue over it. "But I may as well. If I don't get out of here when I graduate, I'll never leave this town."

"Hmm." He pulled up a file on the computer. It was a document Sarah had given him for tonight. It had a D on it. "You didn't do well on your last essay."

"I know. I'm sorry. I've been working to earn extra money and I didn't have time. If you give me a chance, I'll do it again. Better this time."

"That wouldn't be fair to the other students, would it?" He glanced at her over the computer.

"No."

"No, what?" He was starting to get into this. Mary was at his mercy but he had to lure her in. If she ran from here screaming, his days of being a professor were over.

"No, sir." Her lip jutted out again.

"I may be able to help you with the grade, but you'll have to promise me that you won't tell anyone."

"Oh, I won't. I swear, sir." Her eyes sparkled with hope.

He studied her until she squirmed and looked down at her hands which were folded primly in her lap.

"I don't know." His eyes roamed over her. "I don't think you're ready."

"I am, Professor. I'll do anything you ask. I'll fix my paper. Write a new one. Anything."

"I'm taking a big risk by helping you." He tapped his fingers on the desk. "I could lose my job." That was an understatement.

"I swear. I won't say anything to anyone."

"We'll see. I'm going to test you."

"But I haven't studied."

He laughed. "You don't need to study for this kind of test."

"Okay." Her brows knitted in confusion.

"Come here." He scooted his chair away from the desk.

She moved around to his side.

"Sit down."

She glanced at her chair and started to walk over to it.

"No. Not on your chair." He patted his thigh. "Here."

Her face heated but there was fire in her eyes too. His gaze dropped to her bra and there was a slight puckering of her nipples through her white shirt.

"On your lap?"

"Yes, Mary. Unless you want to keep the D."

"No, sir." She turned and sat gingerly on his knees.

He wrapped his arm around her and pulled her closer so her back was flush with his chest, her long, thin thighs resting against his as her ass cradled his erection. She let out a small gasp but didn't move. He scooted the chair closer to the desk.

"Now, I want you to work on your paper."

"Here? Like this?" Her voice was a squeak.

He leaned forward until his lips brushed her ear. "Yes."

She started reading and changing a bit of her essay as he breathed along her ear and neck.

"Do you have a boyfriend?"

"No."

"No, what?"

"No, sir."

"Have you ever had a boyfriend?" He rested his hand on the outside of her thigh, his thumb caressing lightly.

She shook her head, her hands stilling over the keyboard.

"Keep working on your paper." His thumb skimmed under her skirt.

She started typing again, her fingers missing a few keys as she went.

"You've never had a boyfriend? That's hard to believe. You're a very beautiful girl."

"My dad won't let me date." She flushed a bit more.

"Now, that's a shame." He put his other hand against her other leg and gently caressed with both thumbs as he whispered, "Have you ever been kissed, Mary?"

"Once, when I was twelve." Her back was stiff but her hands were trembling and her breathing was ragged.

"Finish your paper, Mary." He swatted her thigh and she jumped but started typing again. "You need to learn to focus. I'll teach you that if you'd like."

She didn't answer.

"Would you like me to teach you? Give you tutoring sessions. Just you and me." He let his lips caress her ear and she shivered.

"I...I don't know."

He pushed his chair back. "You can stand up now."

She didn't move. "Are...is my grade going to be better?"

"No. I'm sorry." He put his hands on her waist and lifted her off his lap. "You didn't pass the test. I can't give you a better grade unless you can learn to focus." He was really enjoying this game.

She faced him. "Please, Professor. I can learn. Please."

His gazed raked down her body. "Show me your underwear."

"What?" She took a step back.

"You have to trust me and do what I say for this to work."

"Oh. I..."

"Either show me your underwear right now, or keep your D and leave. I don't have time for games." Except sex games. Those he had time for.

Her hands drifted to her skirt and raised it. He inhaled deeply, trying to calm his blood, slow his desire but when he saw the white cotton panties already damp he had to grab the arms of the chair so he didn't grab her.

"Good girl. Now, get back on my lap." He patted his thighs.

Her green eyes widened as they landed on his erection, but she dropped her skirt and down. He wrapped his arm around her waist and scooted the chair back to the desk.

"Keep working on your paper. Don't stop, no matter what. If you do, you'll be punished." He leaned forward and whispered in her ear. "Understand?"

"Yes.'

"Yes what?"

"Yes, sir."

"Okay. Now, where were we." He tugged her closer so her ass once again cradled his erection. "Hmm. This isn't comfortable for either of us." He tugged the back of her skirt up so only her underwear and his pants separated his dick from the crease of her ass.

She stilled.

"Keep working." He skimmed his lips up her neck to her ear. "When you were twelve and the boy kissed you, did he use his tongue?"

She shivered. Her nipples had to be little pebbles by now, aching for his touch, his mouth. His thumbs slowly pulled her skirt higher and his fingers now rested against the warm, smooth skin of her outer thigh.

"He...he tried but I wouldn't open my mouth?"

"Why not?"

112

"It seemed gross."

"It's not. Not if it's done correctly." He shifted his hands so his fingers rested on the top of her legs. "Would you like me to show you?"

"I...I don't know." She turned her face toward him a little and it was all the invitation he needed.

Her lips were slightly parted and red as if she'd been nibbling on them. One of his hands came up and cupped the back of her neck as his lips met hers. She kept her mouth tightly sealed even when his tongue skimmed across her seam.

He kissed a trail to her ear. "Open for me, Mary."

"I...I don't..."

He used her words to gain access and he shifted her backward, leaning against his arm as his mouth found hers. At first, she was still and then she tentatively met his tongue, rubbing alongside it. He groaned and pulled her closer, the hand not tangled in her hair starting a slow path to her pussy. He had to touch her. She was wet and ready for him.

She grasped his wrist right before his fingers found her core and she broke the kiss. She struggled to get off his lap but he held her in place, not ready to give up his hard-earned ground just yet.

"Professor, please. I'm not like that. I'm a good girl. I'm a virgin."

He dropped his hands at the slight panic in her voice. Sarah was really working this fantasy. It was arousing and annoying at the same time.

She stood, but didn't move away. She lowered her gaze. "I'm sorry. I can't."

"Don't be sorry." He took her hands. "It's okay." He kissed her knuckles. "I went too fast. It was your first kiss." He smiled, he was a little afraid it was more of a leer but she didn't seem to mind. "What if I promise just to kiss you? That's all. Nothing else." He smiled again. "Well, there will be a little touching but nothing else."

Her eyes dropped to his pants and her face heated. "That'd be okay with you?"

"Yes. Not ideal, but okay."

"And...and I'd get a better grade."

If he were really this professor he'd feel like a heel. "Yes. If you do exactly what I say, you'll get an A on this essay."

"And we won't...." Her eyes dropped to his pants again.

"You'll keep your underwear on and you'll still be a virgin when you leave this office."

"Promise."

"I promise." He crossed his heart.

"I guess that'd be okay then."

"Did you like what we did already?"

Her face turned scarlet.

"Tell me the truth, Mary."

She stared at her hands in his. "Yes." It was barely a whisper.

"Excellent." He tugged her closer and his hands went to the top button on her shirt.

Her eyes flew to his face.

"Only kisses. I promise." He leaned forward and kissed the tiny spot of skin he'd revealed. He moved on to the next one and the next, kissing his way down her chest.

He tasted her warm skin and she inhaled sharply, her knees buckling a little. He unbuttoned the last button, kissing her stomach and dipping his tongue into her navel. Her hands wrapped in his hair and he grabbed her hips. This fantasy was almost over. Time to move on to the real agenda. Sex. He kissed her hips, his fingers grabbing her skirt and underwear. He wanted her naked. Now.

"Professor. Don't. You promised." She yanked on his hair, a little, before dropping her hands to her sides. "Only kisses.'

He took a deep, ragged breath. Apparently, Sarah wasn't done with her game. "Right. Sorry." He opened her shirt and his dick got even harder as unbelievable as that was. She'd gone with the good-girl, plain white bra and it was hot especially with her nipples hard as little pebbles and poking through the cloth.

"This"—his thumbs caressed her nipple and she swayed toward him, pressing against his hand a moment before regaining her balance—"means you like what we're doing, a lot." He tugged her shirt off her shoulders and pulled her closer. He kissed her stomach and her hands fluttered before resting on his shoulders. "That's it Mary, touch me."

"Where?" Her voice was a gasp of passion.

"Where ever you want. Everywhere." His hand wandered up her back and unhooked her bra. She stilled, her fingers grasping his shoulders. "Just kisses. I promise." His lips latched onto her breast and she moaned as he pulled her onto his lap, straddling him.

Her hands went into his hair, pulling his head closer to her breast as he suckled. She tasted so sweet, he'd never tire of sucking her tit. She shifted and rubbed her pussy against him. His hips flexed, matching her rhythm.

"That's it." He said as he moved to her other breast. "See how good we feel together." He pulled one of her hands from his hair and placed it on his cock. "Touch me, Mary. Please." He ran his teeth gently over her nipple as she rubbed him through his pants. It wasn't enough. He needed her skin on his. Shit, he needed to be inside of her. He pulled her mouth to his and reached between them, unzipping his pants. As soon as he was free his finger found her clit and rubbed her through her underwear.

She broke the kiss, gasping. "Oh, oh, Professor."

He rubbed more, shoving his hand inside her panties and inserting his finger inside of her. "Shit, you're so hot. So tight. I've got to…" He lifted her, putting her on her feet. His hands went to her panties to tear them off. Get them out of his way, but she stumbled away from him.

"Professor. You…you said my underwear would stay on. You said I'd still be a virgin."

"Enough Sarah. The game's done." He reached for her but she darted away, racing for the door.

"Oh, no. You're not getting away this time." He ran after her. She was going to pay for this. His hand skimmed across her arm but she slipped away and through the door, slamming it behind her. He grabbed the knob but somehow, she'd managed to get it locked. He slammed his hand against the door. "Let me in. Now. This fantasy is over. I need to fuck you. Right. Now. Right. Bloody. Now."

CHAPTER 3: SARAH

Sarah jumped when Nick hit the door, her heart racing from fear and excitement. He was pissed and horny, so damn horny and so was she. It'd taken everything she had to run out of that room when all she'd wanted was to sink down onto him and let him fill her, but Mary would've been frightened and at that moment, she'd been Mary.

"Damnit, Sarah." He shook the door handle.

"Go back to your desk, Professor." She pulled off her panties—they were soaked with her desire—and tossed them toward her bag. She grabbed her dark green and white panties and pulled them on. These were Lucy's underwear – sexy and sleek.

"I'm done with this game. I mean it." The door rattled. He must have hit it with his shoulder this time.

"Trust me, Nick. Please." She took off her bra and replaced it with one that matched her new panties. She hurried into the bathroom and put her hair up in pigtails.

She grabbed a cherry sucker out of her bag and sucked on it. When it was wet, she rolled it over her lips making them bright red. She splashed on a little perfume and headed to the door, listening. He must've gone back to the desk like she'd asked.

She took a deep breath and unlocked the door, sauntering inside, her hips swinging suggestively as she sucked on the sucker. Nick was once again behind the desk, his face hard with anger and frustrated passion.

She popped the sucker out from between her lips, letting her tongue trail along its round head. "Professor, you can't scream like that. Ms. Applewood works late just down the hallway."

Nick's eyes were black fire as they roamed over her body. "Get over here."

"Oh, did little Mary leave my poor professor hurting." She strolled closer, her eyes going to the huge bulge in his pants that were once again all zipped up. She winced inwardly, it couldn't have felt good shoving that thing back into his pants.

He reached for her but she dodged him and moved to the desk, sliding on top of it.

"Here, Professor." She spread her legs, propping them on the desk so he could see under her skirt.

"You'd better be ready because I'm done fucking around." He stood, unzipping his pants as he shoved her skirt out of the way.

His voice was dark with desire and his words were hot, causing her insides to melt. "Whatever you want, Professor." She sucked on the candy again, her eyes darting to his engorged penis. "Are you sure you want to fuck me right now?" She rolled her tongue around the round sucker. "We could do other things first." Her eyes locked with his and then her gaze went to his cock and she licked the sucker again, sticking it into her mouth and sucking.

His nostrils flared. "Later. I'd never last." He grabbed her panties, yanking them off and letting them fall to the floor. He tugged her closer to the edge of the desk and moved between her thighs. His dick was so hard and hot against her that she arched her back to get closer, rubbing against him. He positioned himself and she froze.

"Condom." She put her hand between them, trying to block her wet passage.

"No, baby." He kissed the side of her neck, his open mouth trailing to her ear. "Please, I need to feel you."

"Condom." She dropped the sucker and shoved his chest with her other hand. She wasn't budging on this.

His mouth came down on hers as he tried to pry her hand away so he could enter her. She shifted away from him.

"Damnit, Nick. Put on a condom." She was so hot for him but she wouldn't take this chance. It was too big of a risk.

"Fuck. Fine." He stepped back and tore open a condom, sliding it over his dick. He moved between her legs and pulled her thighs farther apart. In one quick movement, he thrust inside of her. She gasped at the intrusion, so hard and yet, so good. Her arms wrapped around his neck, holding on while he slammed into her hard and fast.

"Fuck, you're so wet and tight. Fuck Sarah." He

withdrew and filled her again.

Her legs locked around his waist, pulling him closer. She needed this. She needed him. He pushed into her, his lips pressed against her neck as she pushed against him, meeting him thrust for thrust. "Harder, Nick, please."

He nipped her neck and shifted position.

"Oh, yes, right there." It was that spot. That special place that only he found. She closed her eyes, her legs tightening and her pelvis thrusting against him, as her inner muscles clamped down on his cock, wanting to keep him inside.

He reached between them, his fingers finding her nipple. He bit her neck as he thrust into her and pinched her tit. She exploded against him. Everything disappearing but him. He was the only solid thing in her universe and her body clung to him—hands, arms, legs and pussy.

"Sarah." He groaned as he came, his dick twitching inside of her before he collapsed, his breath hot and heavy against her neck. "Fuck me," he gasped.

She turned her head, kissing the side of his face. "I just did."

He smiled against her neck. "You sure did and we're going to have to do this professor fantasy again. Maybe a couple of times."

She ran her hand up his back, wishing he were naked. "Good because you still need to meet Ms. Applewood, the lonely, uptight librarian."

"I don't know if I can handle another female in this fantasy." He leaned up and pushed the hair off her face. "But I can't wait to try." He kissed her, soft but with the promise of heat to come.

Book 4

Master - Slave Fantasy

CHAPTER 1: SARAH

Sarah hurried down the hallway to the hotel room. This was their weekday visit and she was running late. Maisie had gotten stuck in traffic. Nick wasn't going to be happy that he wouldn't get his hour. She opened the door and stepped inside.

"Take off your clothes."

Nick's voice came out of the darkness, all rough and male and immediately wetness pooled between her legs. She wanted him right here and now, but she'd delay. It was always fun to play.

"I'm sorry. I must have the wrong room."

"Does it matter?" He turned on the table lamp. It cast shadows on his narrow face, highlighting his hungry, dark eyes.

She appreciated that Nick was smart enough to pick up on her game. Her fingers went to the button on her blouse, teasing. "You…you must be expecting someone."

"You."

"I was supposed to meet my friend."

"You can do that later." He took a drink from the glass in his hand. "Unbutton your blouse."

"I…I don't know you."

"So."

"Who were you expecting? Your wife? Girlfriend?"

"I paid for an escort. If you're not it, you'll do."

She gasped. "I'm not a prostitute."

He stood, all slow grace and masculinity. "Neither am I." He strolled over to her until his chest brushed against hers with each breath. "Unbutton your blouse."

Her hands trembled, but she only rolled the button between her fingers.

He leaned down and kissed her neck, making his way to her ear. "Please." He rubbed his erection against her belly.

"I…I don't usually do this."

He moved back a few inches, his eyes on her fingers. "I know."

She unbuttoned the first button. Her fingers trailed against her skin as she moved to the next one. His gaze was hot, almost a caress. When she had the second button undone he leaned down and kissed her exposed skin, flicking her with his tongue and then sucking. She grabbed his head, wanting those lips and that mouth on her breasts. He pushed her hands out of the way and unhooked a button.

His fingers fumbled on the next one so he clasped her shirt and yanked. Buttons shot across the room.

"Nick! What am I going…"

He shoved her bra up and his mouth latched onto her nipple, sucking hard and stopping her words and all thought, except more. She held him to her and moaned as she rocked against his erection.

"Fuck, Sarah," he said against her breast as his hands shoved her skirt up to her waist. "I have to be inside you when you do that. I have to." He ripped her underwear off and lifted her legs, wrapping them around his hips as he pressed her against the door.

"Do what?" She caressed his neck, stopping herself, just barely, from shoving his face back to her breasts.

He unzipped his pants and slipped on a condom. His fingers skimmed across her pussy. "You're drenched. For me." His lips came down on hers as he shoved into her. She gasped into his mouth as he stretched her, filling her with pleasure and a hint of pain. He always felt good, but the first time each night was the best. The fullness of him, the length, the way he stretched her, forcing her to accept him, all of him—it was perfect. She clasped her inner muscles, clinging to him.

"Shit, baby. Do that again." He pulled out and slid back in and she tightened her legs around his waist, her arms wrapping around his back, holding him to her with every muscle she had.

He moved his head to her breast and licked her nipple, a soft caress of his rough tongue. She moaned, her hand going to his head. It wasn't enough and she guided him closer to her breast. He smiled, his teeth against her skin and she shivered. If he nipped her, she'd come.

"Please, Nick."

He licked all around her nipple as she tried to force his mouth to her breast and then he was there. Right where she needed him. His mouth sucking on her breast sending lightning through her veins and causing her hips to rock against him.

"Fuck, that's it." He said before sucking harder.

Her back arched, smashing her breast into his face and her pussy tightened around him as he thrust in and out.

"Oh, Nick. Please…"

He increased his pace, shoving into her harder and harder as he sucked her nipple. Her body trembled at the onslaught, tightening even more. She was going to come. She was almost there and then his teeth grazed her nipple and she screamed clamping down on him and holding him tight. He thrust into her twice more and groaned his release against her breast.

They stayed like that for a long time, or at least it seemed like a long time. She was still wrapped around him, her back pressed to the door and his face resting against her breast and then he withdrew from her and she sighed. She hated when he pulled out. She could live with his dick inside of her, filling her and making her feel whole again. She dropped her legs to the floor. Those were dangerous thoughts. This was a fling. Sex. Nothing else.

She pulled her bra down to cover her breasts and started to button her shirt but most of the buttons were gone. She straightened her skirt. "I'll see you Saturday."

"What?" He tucked his cock back into his pants

and zipped them.

She kissed his cheek. "It was great, but I have to go."

"You have an hour."

She blinked. "We won't have sex again. You'll sleep…"

"I'm not tired."

She bent to pick up her underwear and he grabbed them before walking to the couch.

"Hey, I need those." She glanced down at her shirt. "Actually, you can keep them, but I need to borrow a shirt or jacket. I can't walk out of here like this."

"Why don't you keep clothes here? I have the place for three more weeks."

"Two and a half." She wanted to pull back the words. She didn't want him to realize she was counting the days, dreading the end of their affair.

"Yeah." He didn't sound happy and that made her glad.

"Can I borrow a shirt?" She headed for the bedroom to get one.

"No."

She stopped. "No?"

He grabbed her hand and pulled her down to his lap. "Yes, but not now. When the hour is up."

She sat stiffly, not wanting to get comfortable. She couldn't afford to get comfortable around him. This was going to end and it was better if it ended on her terms. Adam had taught her that.

"Relax." He pulled her against his chest, her head on his shoulder.

"If we're not going to have sex again and you're not going to sleep, what are we going to do." She fought her desire to accept this closeness, to cherish this gift, but it'd be her undoing. "We can't talk. Not about anything personal so that leaves almost everything out."

"We can just sit." His hand stroked her hair and he kissed her forehead. "Just stay with me for a bit. I promise we'll both go when the hour is up."

She shouldn't but she couldn't help herself. His heart beat steady under her ear and his arms surrounded her. She'd believe his body's lie – the lie of safety – for now. She relaxed against him and sighed. She was in so much trouble.

CHAPTER 2: SARAH

"Sarah, wake up."

Adam shook her but she snuggled closer, burying her face in his chest. He smelled nice—a hint of some woodsy cologne and male.

"Baby, come on." His arms tightened around her and his dick, already prodding against her thigh, hardened a little more. "You're not making this easy." He kissed the top of her head. "You have to wake up. It's time for you to go."

She didn't want to go. She was comfortable in his arms, but this wasn't Adam. It wasn't Adam's voice and Adam never smelled like this.

"If you don't get up now, I'm going to carry you into the bedroom and fuck you until you scream." His hand wandered from her waist to her thighs, moving slowly between them.

Adam never talked to her like that. He wouldn't.

He hadn't wanted her. Not at the end, but Nick did. Nick was hard for her, waiting for her and she wanted him, but she couldn't stay. She moaned as his fingers move under her skirt and brushed softly against her pussy.

"Don't. I have to go," she said against his chest before turning and climbing off his lap. "Sorry."

His gaze was already hot with passion and the bulge in his pants promised she wouldn't be disappointed. She bit her lip, wanting him so bad but she couldn't do that to Tank. He'd think she'd abandoned him like Adam had.

"You'd better go now, or you won't be leaving for"—his gazed caressed her breasts, covered only by the bra since the buttons of her shirt were gone—"at least ten minutes."

She laughed. "A whole ten minutes. You're a charmer you are."

"You like it fast and hard."

"I do." Her eyes roamed down his chest to his pants. "But I have to go." She took a step toward the bedroom when he grabbed her hand, stopping her. "You said I could borrow a shirt."

"If you go in the bedroom, you aren't coming out tonight." He let go of her hand, a challenge in his eyes.

She wanted to take him up on the game. She was more than eager to play, but she couldn't. "Will you get me a shirt then?" She glanced down at her chest. "I can't leave like this."

"Chicken." He pulled his shirt off and handed it to her.

"Thanks." She put it on and headed for the door, stopping before she opened it. "Why did you wake me?

I'm glad you did, but why?"

"For our game this Saturday, you need to trust me. Completely. I figured this proves that no matter how much I want it, I won't do anything you don't want."

A wave of lust flowed through her, turning into liquid between her thighs. She already trusted him too much and she was eager to play his slave.

CHAPTER 3: SARAH

When Sarah arrived at the hotel Saturday night, the room was empty. A note waited for her, taped to the couch.

Your costume is in the bedroom. Put it on. All of it. And wait for me.

Write your safeword on the back of this paper and leave it on the couch. Make sure I can read your writing.

Nick

Sarah scribbled her safeword down and went into the bedroom. Excitement raced through her with a hint of fear. She'd never done anything like this before and she was nervous. She trusted him, but she was going to be at his mercy. Tonight, she was his slave—a young girl, little to no experience who was sold to him. Her panties were

130

already wet and she felt empty and aching for him. She'd had no idea she'd be into this submissive shit.

The bed was made, as usual, but there were restraints at the headboard and the posts at the bottom of the bed. Her stomach twisted as more wetness pooled between her legs. Did she trust him enough to allow him to tie her up? She'd never been restrained before. Adam hadn't liked games like that, or if he had, he hadn't played them with her. Their sex life, the little they'd had, had been normal, no wilder than a couple of different positions.

She'd get dressed and worry about the restraints later. He'd been nice enough to play her fantasy. She'd at least give his a try. If she got scared or didn't like something, she had her safeword and she trusted him to listen to her. He'd been nothing but kind so far. Kind and sexy and oh so delicious.

She stripped out of her jeans and T-shirt, tossing them over a chair and picked up the clothes from the bed. It was Nick's shirt. She stilled as she noticed a shackle attached to the one leg of the bed with a sticky note on it.

Put me on too.

He wanted her to chain herself before he even got here. She glanced around but there was no key in sight. She slipped into the shirt and searched the bedroom but couldn't find the key. She picked up the shackle. It was lined with silk so it wouldn't scrape her skin. She put it around her ankle but didn't lock it. If something happened and he didn't show up, there was no way she was going to get caught like this by the maid. Plus, she had to be home for Tank.

If Nick didn't like it too bad. She'd chain herself as soon as he got here. She sat on the bed and waited. It seemed like forever. She unhooked her leg and went into the living room. She poured herself a drink and flopped on the couch, turning on the TV.

She'd almost finished her drink when she heard the click of the door. She turned off the TV and rushed into the bedroom, hooking the shackle around her ankle but hesitated before latching it. "Nick, is that you?"

He walked into the bedroom. He was dressed in black dress slacks and a white button down shirt. He looked like the professional he probably was. His face was stern and his black hair windblown. His eyes roamed over her, hot with desire, until they landed on her ankle.

"Close the shackle or do you want to be punished?"

She swallowed as she latched the restraint. She was stuck now, for better or worse.

"Stand up."

She did, suddenly nervous and yet excited. Her eyes wandered to his groin where the beginning of a bulge was forming.

He studied her. "Pretty enough but you seem to have a problem obeying."

"I'm sorry—"

"Did I tell you to speak?"

"No." She bit her lip and made a face because she probably should've shook her head.

There was a spark of amusement in his eyes before they narrowed again. It wasn't much but it made her feel better. This was still Nick.

"Come forward."

She moved toward him.

"Stop. Take off your shirt."

Her hands trembled slightly from excitement as she unbuttoned the shirt. With his dark eyes watching her and her complete submission to him, she was getting more turned on by the minute. By the gleam in his eyes, he liked her nervousness so she played it up, taking her time removing the shirt. His nostrils were flaring a bit by the time she was done. She left the shirt hanging open, covering more of her body than it revealed.

"Take it off."

She shrugged and the cloth slid to the floor.

"Why are you wearing a bra and underwear? Was that part of the outfit I left for you?" He walked around her, slowly.

"No. Sorry—"

"No, Master." He whispered in her ear, his hot breath making her shiver with want.

"No, Master," she repeated.

He moved in front of her. "You're sorry a lot."

She didn't know what to say to that.

"Didn't I tell you to get dressed and wait for me?"

"Yes." At his raised eyebrow she said, "Yes, Master."

"Then why were you watching television and drinking my liquor? Did I say you could do that?"

"No. No, Master. I'm sorry, Ma—"

In a flash, she was in his arms. In two steps, they were at the bed and he was sitting and she was lying over his legs. His hand came down hard on her butt.

"Ouch! Hey."

"Do not speak unless I give you permission." His hand caressed her bottom, sliding down to her thighs and between them, but not touching where she most needed him to. She relaxed a bit on his legs. "Do you understand?" His fingers trailed down the crack of her ass.

"Yes. Yes, Master." She squirmed a little, wanting him to touch her. She was already wet and aching for him.

He slapped her ass again.

"Ouch!"

He stood her up, but stayed sitting on the bed. "Silence."

She nodded rubbing her backside. She wasn't sure about the spankings. Part of her had been turned on, a lot, by the helpless position but not by the actual hitting.

"Take off your bra. I want to see what I paid for."

She unhooked her bra and let it drop, her nipples were already hard and pointing at him, begging him to taste them, suck them.

"Now, your panties." His voice was rougher and the bulge in his pants had grown considerably.

She shimmied out of them, kicking them off her feet.

His eyes raked over her body, sending shivers of warmth racing through her. She wanted him now.

"What's your name?"

"Sarah," she said, not in the mood to answer to something else tonight.

"Sarah, I think we'll get along fine as long as you can learn to obey." He started unbuttoning his shirt. "I'm a kind master, if you do what I say."

She remained quiet, her eyes following his hands as they exposed more and more of his wonderful chest.

"Go into the bathroom and draw a bath for me."

"The chain, Master."

He pulled a key from his pocket. "Give me your leg."

She lifted her leg and he took her ankle, positioning her foot so it rested against his groin and opened her up for his view. His eyes darkened as he stared at her pussy and she couldn't help it, she got wetter. She'd be dripping in a minute.

She wanted to rub her toes along his length but she was supposed to be an unwilling slave so she remained still but it wasn't easy. His hands were warm and strong, caressing her foot. She shifted slightly, trying to press her thighs together. She needed pressure between her legs. He smirked a little and unlocked the cuff. She started to move her foot but hesitated. There was something expectant about the way he was watching her.

He smiled as his fingers caressed her calf, trailing past her knee. "Good girl. You waited for permission. Good girls get rewarded." He leaned forward and kissed her inner thigh, his mouth open and wet and she shivered, her hands reaching for his head to guide him to the place that wept for his touch, but stopped herself, dropping her hands back at her sides.

He breathed along her slit and a whimper escaped her lips. His hot breath felt good but not substantial enough. She needed his tongue or fingers or cock.

He sat up. "Go. Get my bath ready."

Her legs wobbled as she walked into the bathroom.

She wanted him so badly. She bent over the claw-footed tub, turning on the water. She felt his presence more than heard him. He was behind her, close enough so she could feel the heat from his body. She forced herself not to turn and grab him. She had to get her head into this game or he wouldn't enjoy it. Well, he'd enjoy it but not as much as if she acted how he wanted her to.

"You're a very beautiful woman. I'm glad I bought you." His hand rested on her back, pushing her gently downward, until her hands were braced on the other side of the tub. He ran a piece of ice down her spine. She stiffened at the cold but his lips soon followed the ice, his mouth hot and wet contrasting with the cold. She moved her legs apart, giving him better access and she hoped a hint, but he continued kissing her back, going not farther than her ass.

"Nick, please." She couldn't take this anymore.

He froze. "What did you call me?"

"Master, please."

"That's better." He slapped her butt, hard.

She jumped but her pussy quivered for him, wondering what it'd feel like to get a slap like that when he was inside her. His hands moved to her hips, pulling her ass flush against him, his hard length pressing into her backside.

"Should I forgo the bath and get straight to the fucking?" He rubbed himself along her and she bit her lip to stop from moaning.

Her entire body screamed for her to say yes, but this was his fantasy and she wanted to please him. "No, Master. Please. I'll do anything but please leave me be."

He stilled, his hands loosening. "Stand up."

She straightened but didn't turn around, hoping she hadn't made a mistake and ruined his game.

"You don't understand." He leaned close, whispering in her ear. "I bought you. I own you. I will fuck you."

She shivered. It was because she couldn't wait but it could've been in fear. "Please, Master. I...I don't—"

He stepped back. "Turn around."

She turned, keeping her eyes downcast to try and hide her desire.

"Are you a virgin?"

She shook her head.

"Good. Virgins are horrible fucks."

"I...I've only...once."

"Damn. I figured you'd been ridden hard. Innocents usually cost more." He lifted her chin. "What else have you done?"

She shook her head. "Nothing. I...only that one time."

"Did you like it?"

"No. It hurt."

"It'll only hurt this time if you want it to."

Her eyes flew to his. "Why would I want it to hurt?" That was a legitimate question.

He leaned so his lips were at her ear. "Pain and pleasure go together. I'll make sure to teach you that."

"Please, Master, can't I serve you some other way. I don't—"

"Enough. Turn off the water."

She did.

"On your knees," he said.

She knelt in front of him, her gaze wandering up his muscular thighs to his cock. He was so close she could smell his arousal—musky, earthy male. She wanted to unzip his pants but she was his slave and this was his fantasy, so she waited for his command.

"Take off my pants."

She almost smiled but she remembered she should be pretending to be nervous. She was this man's property.

"Now. My next punishment won't be a swat on your ass."

She made her hands shake as she unbuttoned his pants and then slowly unzipped them. She tried to look nervous but she was sure her eyes were filled with anticipation. She slid his pants and underwear down his slim hips being careful of his rock-hard penis.

He walked over to the tub, his cock leading the way. He glanced at her as he lowered himself into the bath. He nodded at his empty glass on the bathroom counter. "Get me another drink."

Her heart stuttered in disappointment and she almost glared at the smug look on his face. He knew exactly what she'd wanted and he'd denied her. Well, she'd play that game too. She went into the living room and poured him a scotch.

"Bring in a chair," he yelled from the bathroom.

She grabbed a chair from the table before returning.

"You're doing much better at following commands. It seems a little spanking helps." He held out his hand and she gave him his drink. "Wash me."

She started to move the chair over by the tub.

138

"No. Leave the chair where it is. Lean over the tub as you wash me."

If she did that, her breasts would be at face level. Her nipples hardened to the point of pain. She picked up the wash cloth and soap and moved to the tub.

She positioned herself behind his back and dipped the cloth into the water by his side. He was leaning against the tub, sipping his drink. She wrung out the rag and soaped it up. She started on his shoulders. His body was so different than hers, hard and strong. She ran the cloth over his skin and used her fingers to massage the tension from his neck and shoulders.

"Ah, Sarah, you're very good at this." He leaned forward, giving her better access and she trailed her fingers down his spine, making little circles at each juncture. She put pressure with her thumbs and he moaned. She'd paid attention during her massages, although she'd never had a sensual one like this.

She finished his back and walked over to the counter and got the shampoo. She held it up and he nodded, his eyes hooded as he studied her nakedness. Her nipples puckered as his eyes raked over them and he smiled, pure male, pure masculine and her body responded by becoming wet again and ready for him.

She grabbed the cup that was on the bathroom counter and carried that along with the shampoo and conditioner to the tub. She ran water in the cup and started to walk behind him, but he leaned forward, his face even with her breasts.

"This'll be easier." He tipped his head, his cheek brushing against her nipple and she couldn't help the small

moan that escaped her lips. She wanted more than his
cheek, but this was his fantasy, his game and even if it
killed her, she'd play.

She soaked his hair and then added the shampoo
massaging his scalp. His hair was thick and heavy and felt
glorious under her fingers but she wanted to get on with
washing the rest of him, so she hurried and rinsed his hair,
adding the conditioner and rinsing again. She went behind
him, re-soaped the rag and started on his arms. She loved
his muscles—the strength it took for him to hold himself
above her and plow into her over and over again. These
arms, these muscles should get a medal. She smiled
slightly. Maybe the medal should go to his penis but the
arms deserved something.

She scrubbed his chest, her hands lingering around
his nipples making him suck in his breath. She placed the
washcloth on the side of the tub. "Done, Master."

"You are not done."

"Please Master, I…I don't want—"

"Wash all of me, Sarah or do you want another
spanking?"

She did but this wasn't the time. He was extremely
aroused, his cock jutting below the water. "No, Master."
She picked up the wash cloth and moved to the front of the
tub where she took her time, washing his feet, calves and
thighs, touching everything but what he wanted her to
touch. She was really beginning to enjoy this teasing.

"Enough, Sarah."

Her eyes flew to his. He couldn't stop now. She
hadn't touched him yet.

"All of me." He raised his brow and she almost

sighed in relief but instead she cast her eyes down and tried to flush but it wasn't easy to turn red on command.

She let her hand, with the washcloth, glide into the water to his thigh and then upward. His breath caught in his throat as she wrapped her hand around his dick and began to rub up and down. "Like this, Master?"

He tipped back his head. "Yes. Exactly like that but tighten your grip."

She did and then she moved the washcloth to his balls while her other hand stroked him in long, firm strokes, letting her thumb caress the tip on each stroke.

"Fuck." He grabbed her hand, stopping her. "Enough." He stood and got out of the tub. "Dry me."

He was naked and painfully aroused and she was wet and ready. It wouldn't be long now. She grabbed a large towel and ran it over his face and down his chest and back, not spending too much time anywhere. None of those body parts – although glorious—were where she wanted to focus. She stepped closer, and wrapped her towel covered hand around his penis. He stared down at her, his breathing shallow and his eyes black.

He took the towel from her and gently pushed her back a step. He grabbed the chair, pulling it close and sat, dropping the towel on the floor. "On your knees."

She could barely contain her grin as she knelt between his knees, his erection bobbing in front of her.

"Suck me."

"Master...I..." She licked her lips and he inhaled sharply. "I don't. I've never."

"It's easy enough. Put your mouth around my dick and suck."

She leaned forward, touching him only with the tips of her lips.

"Open your mouth and take me inside."

She licked off the musky pre-cum and then sucked him into her mouth, running her tongue along him.

"Suck." His hand tangled in her hair and he shoved her down on him.

She opened more, taking as much of him inside as she could. He groaned and his hips thrust upward when she moved downward on him. His penis hit the back of her throat but she managed not to gag. He was lost in the pleasure and she didn't want to stop him so she sucked harder.

His hand yanked on her hair, jerking her off his cock. She expected him to grab her and fuck her but his hand replaced her mouth and he stroked himself.

"Shut your eyes," he gasped.

"What?" She was confused.

"Fuck. I'm coming." His other hand came out and covered her eyes as he ejaculated on her face. His cum hitting her in hot, gooey streams. His hand dropped away from her but she didn't move. His sperm was dripping off her face and she felt so...ashamed...so humiliated. A small sob slipped past her lips.

"Sarah," his voice was soft.

"Yes...Ma...Master." She was trying hard not to cry.

"Fuck that. Sarah, look at me." He was kneeling by her but she still didn't open her eyes. "I can't believe I'm going to say this, but *cat litter*. Your safeword. We're not playing right now." He brushed her hair away from her face, wiping off some of his cum. "Look at me."

She shook her head. If she did, he'd see the tears in her eyes.

"Damnit, open your eyes and look at me." He shook her gently.

She did.

"Oh, honey. I'm sorry. Don't cry." He grabbed the wash cloth and wiped her face before picking her up and pulling her onto his lap as he sat on the chair. "I didn't hurt you, did I?"

She shook her head. Not physically.

"Then why are you crying? If you don't like facials, we won't do them. Okay?"

She nodded.

He kissed her cheek. "If it didn't hurt, will you tell me why you're crying?"

She rested her head against his shoulder. "Why did you want to humiliate me? I never did any..." She sobbed. She'd trusted him, but he was no different than Adam, not at the core where it mattered. He didn't care if he hurt her.

"Oh, baby no. I didn't want to humiliate you. That's not why I did that." He tipped her chin up and stared at her until she met his gaze. "I'd never do that. Never."

"Then why?"

"Because it turns me on, but not because I see it as humiliation but"—his thumbs caressed her cheek—"you're so beautiful and...this is kind of my way of making you mine."

"Branding me."

He grinned sheepishly. "Kind of, yeah. I like to see

my cum on you." His eyes darted to her breasts. "On your body and your face. It's hot."

"You really like it." She didn't understand that at all.

"Yeah. You do it to me too."

"What? No..."

"When I eat you out, my face is full of you. Even after I wash, I swear I can still smell you on me."

Now, her face heated. "I'm sorry. I—"

"Don't be sorry. I love it. It's you and it proves you're mine...at least for that moment."

"Oh." She wasn't sure what to say.

"But this...all this is for us to experiment and do things we both like. So, we won't do facials again."

"I..I...thank you." She met his eyes. "I might be oaky with it later, but I'm not sure yet."

"Take your time." He stood, placing her on the chair. He removed the stopper from the tub. "I'll be right back." He returned with a drink for her and another for him. He plugged the tub and began filling it with water again. "Are you okay with me cumming on other parts of you, besides your face? If you're not, that's okay, but I need to know."

She took a large gulp of her drink. "Yeah. I guess that'd be okay."

He smiled and kissed her. "That's my girl." He took her hand. "Come on. It's time for your bath."

"Yes, Master." She stood.

"No. We're done with that for tonight." He picked her up and gently placed her in the tub. He knelt at the side and soaped the rag. He kissed her. There was no hunger to it, only comfort and a hint of attraction, a hint that there would be more soon.

He washed her face and then her hair, massaging her scalp. She tipped back her head, his fingers were magic. He rinsed her hair and then picked up the rag, trailing it over her as his hands worked out the tension in her shoulders. She sipped her drink and drifted in and out, feeling nothing but the soothing caress from his strong hands, until they roamed around to her front. His touch became less about comfort and more about arousal as he washed her breasts, playing particular attention to her nipples. The rough cloth making them pucker. She squeezed her legs together, eager for his touch elsewhere. Men should have more hands.

He kissed her cheek and she felt him smile as his hand drifted lower, missing her pussy and massaging her thigh. She couldn't help it, she moved toward his hand.

"I have to wash your other leg first, baby." There was amusement in his voice. "Patience."

She turned and kissed him. "Please, Nick."

He deepened the kiss as he rubbed the cloth over her mound. She moaned into his mouth and he stroked back and forth, the cloth making an incredible friction and then the cloth was gone and it was only his lovely hand. He dipped his finger inside her and thrust. She dropped her drink and grabbed his arms, not to stop him but to hold on. She'd been so ready before that she was almost gone now.

"That's it, baby." His other hand caressed her breast as he thrust another finger inside her and his thumb caressed her hard little nub.

"Oh, oh Nick." She was almost there, she pushed

against his hand. She wanted more but she was so close.

He lowered his other hand and gave her clit a tiny pinch, sending electricity shooting through her. Her hips flew up, rocking and he kept thrusting as she rode his hand.

When she was done, and had flopped back against the tub, he lifted her out, steadying her on her feet before drying her with a fresh, soft towel. He carried her into the bedroom and placed her on the bed, getting in beside her and pulling her close.

CHAPTER 4: SARAH

When Sarah woke, Nick was leaning up on an elbow watching her.

"You're back." He grinned, obviously proud that he'd knocked her out.

She couldn't help but smile at him. "Yeah." She trailed her finger over his bicep. "What time is it?"

"About ten."

"Early still." She was glad. She'd have regretted sleeping the night away. She kissed his chest. "What do you propose we do?"

His eyes darkened but he only stretched out on his back, pulling her close. "Tell me why the facial bothered you so much?"

"I already told you I felt humiliated." She stiffened in his arms but he didn't let go.

"I get that, but you were really upset." He turned on his side so he could look her in the face. "Has someone humiliated you before?"

"Not like that. It wasn't sexual." She frowned as
he continued to stare at her, expecting more. "It's personal,
Nick and we're not supposed to do personal."

"Fuck Ethan and his rules." He got out of bed.

She missed his warmth, the safety she felt in his
arms.

He grabbed the sheet, wrapping it around his waist.
"I want to know what happened to you. I don't give a shit
about the rules. We're past that. Aren't we?"

Her breath hitched in her throat. She needed the
rules. They were all that was keeping her heart safe. "It's
nothing. Really."

"Then tell me." He sat next to her.

He'd been so kind and so dear. She couldn't deny
him anything right now. "Okay. I'll tell you but no
questions afterwards."

"Fine." His eyes narrowed.

"Promise?" She didn't want twenty questions from
him and there'd be more after she told him.

"As long as you tell me what happened."

"I will." This wasn't going to be easy. "I think
you're going to be disappointed. It's nothing like you're
probably thinking."

"Just tell me."

She sighed. "I was in love with a man."

"Figures."

"It was a long time ago. We started dating in high
school." She stared past Nick and into her memories. "He
was my first real boyfriend."

"He was your first?"

She blinked, seeing Nick again. "Yes."

"And he hurt you."

She touched his hand that was fisted in the blankets. "Not like that. Let me explain. Things were good. Great even and then we graduated. Adam joined the army and I went to college. I saw him again after basic training and…and things were different. He was different."

"How?"

"He didn't want to spend much time with me. He hung out with his friends a lot and I couldn't understand. I still loved him, but…" She wiped a tear off her cheek. "I was stupid."

"We're all stupid at that age." He cupped her face in his hands and gave her a soft kiss.

"Adam left again and I wrote to him every day. He didn't write back often, but he did write me. And then he was coming home on leave. He called and said we needed to talk."

"Ouch." Nick moved onto the bed and pulled her close.

"Yeah. I should've known what that meant." She laughed a little. She'd been so naive. "But I didn't. I was so excited, I thought he was going to propose."

"Oh, shit." He kissed the top of her head.

"It gets worse."

"I'm sorry." He lifted her chin and kissed her lips, gently. "But I'm glad he didn't propose."

She smiled up at him and almost said me too, but the words froze in her throat. She wasn't glad. She wasn't. She'd loved Adam. She still loved Adam. She took a deep breath and looked back at her hand as it caressed Nick's wide chest. "I met with his mother to help plan his surprise party."

"You didn't tell his mom about your assumption, did you?"

"No. Not at first."

He groaned.

"She brought it up. She said Adam had told her he had big news. She was sure he was going to propose and that made me more sure."

He sighed and ran his hand up and down her back.

"We threw a huge party. His mom wasn't good at keeping secrets so pretty much everyone knew Adam was going to propose to me, and I was going to say yes." She closed her eyes, pushing the humiliation away.

"How bad was it?"

"Pretty bad. He arrived with another woman." She couldn't stop the tears. It still hurt. "They'd obviously been together for a while. They were quite comfortable around each other." She laughed but it was hollow. "She was the surprise for his mother."

"Asshole."

"He wasn't an asshole. He was a young guy in love." But not with her.

"He was still an asshole. He should've told you."

"He did. He talked to Lisa, his girlfriend, and then came over to me. He tried to get me to go outside with him, to talk, but I refused to move. I knew he'd make me leave and I didn't want to do that. I should've left but I felt so stupid. Everyone knew…" She took a deep breath. "It was so humiliating."

He kissed the top of her head.

"Since I wouldn't go outside with him, he apologized, but he said he was in love with Lisa. Then, he went back to his new girlfriend and she looked at me with pity. Not smugness or victory but pity. I hated her. If she'd been cocky or nasty it wouldn't have been so bad…and then everyone else looked at me like that too. They tried to hide it, but it was there, lurking in their sad eyes and kind words."

"That son-of-a-bitch." His arm tightened, smashing her against him.

"No. He was young and I was stupid. I thought we'd be together forever. I ignored all the signs that he'd lost interest in me."

"He was still an asshole. He could've handled it better."

"I could've too." She hadn't told him the worst part and she wasn't going to.

"I'm sorry that happened to you." He rolled on his side and hugged her.

"I've never talked to anyone about that night." She'd been too embarrassed to tell her sister although Maisie had heard. Everyone in town had heard.

"I'm glad you told me." He kissed the top of her head again.

She looked up at him. He was concerned, truly concerned. She kissed him because she just couldn't not do it. Her tongue glided across his lips. He opened his mouth and his cock stirred against her leg, but a moment later he pulled away. She didn't want to stop. Her hand drifted down his chest but he caught it before she could touch him.

"Sarah," his voice was raspy with desire.

"Please Nick. I told you. Now, make me forget."

"Are you sure?"

"Yes." She kissed him and before she knew it she was on her back.

He hopped out of the bed, grabbed her ankles and pulled her to the edge. He knelt and kissed her knee.

She leaned up on her elbows, aroused by the sight of his dark head moving closer and closer to her cunt. She spread her legs wider and he looked up at her, grinning.

"Eager little beaver aren't you."

She laughed at his joke but the sound died on her lips as his tongue darted inside of her. Hot and warm and strong. He withdrew, licking along the sides as he spread her thighs wider. His tongue danced around her little bud and she bucked, trying to shift so he touched her where she needed him, but he kept dodging her needs, teasing her. She reached for his head but he snatched her hands, holding them in place at her waist.

She couldn't take any more. She needed him now. "Nick. Please. Fuck me." She tightened her legs, squeezing his head between her thighs. His mouth came down on her clit and she moaned, the suction taking her to the edge. He thrust his tongue inside of her, over and over. Her body tensed. She was almost there. Her hips started to buck but he pulled back and flipped her over.

"On your hands and knees."

She knelt spreading her legs wide. One of his hands caressed her ass as he opened a condom and then he was there, pushing inside of her, filling her and stretching her. She moaned and he pulled out and shoved in as she pushed back against him. He did it over and over. Her passage getting wetter and wetter, a sucking, slapping sound filled the room as his balls knocked against her thighs.

His fingers dug into her hips but she barely felt it, so lost in her passion and his thrusting, the feel of him inside her hard and long and hitting her in the exact right spot.

"There, please." She panted. "Right…there."

His hand moved to her stomach and as he thrust he pushed upward with his hand, making sure that his dick hit her g-spot hard. She screamed and came, her hips twitching in release and her inner muscles clenching onto him. He pounded into her again and again before groaning his release and flopping down on her back.

They stayed like that for several moments before he crawled into the bed, pulling her close and tucking her by his side.

"I'd never humiliate you. Never." He kissed the top of her head and fell asleep.

CHAPTER 5: NICK

When Nick woke, Sarah was gone. He sat up in bed running his hand through his hair. He cared about her. A lot. He had no idea when that'd happened or even how. Six weeks was never going to be enough. He turned on the light. There was a note on the night stand. He opened it.

> *Nick,*
> *I'm sorry about ruining your fantasy*
> *tonight. If you want, we can continue it next week.*
> *I believe that Sarah the Slave has escaped her*
> *Master but he's tracked her down in her apartment.*
> *How she's punished is up to you.*
> *Sarah.*

Nick grinned as his cock twitched. He was going to have to bring some toys next week.

Book 5

Punishment Fantasy

CHAPTER 1: SARAH

Sarah opened the hotel door and hesitated a moment before entering. The room was dark. Nick usually arrived before her, but he hadn't last week and as far as she knew they were playing the Master and Slave again tonight, so…She touched the wall, looking for the light switch as she stepped inside the room. Someone grabbed her arm, twisting it behind her back and shoving her against the door as he closed it. Panic raced through her and she kicked at him, struggling to get free but he had her other arm and was using his body to hold her flush against the door.

"Please, I don't have much money but…" This had to be Nick. Oh God, please let it be Nick or let him get here and save her. She knew better than to enter a dark room or house, especially without Tank waiting inside for her.

"I don't want your money. Or should I say my money."

It was Nick's words hot against her ear and she relaxed a little. He pulled her arm farther upwards, his way of reminding her of their game.

"Ouch, please."

"Please what?"

"Please Master, don't hurt me."

"You ran away from me." He nipped her ear and she shivered. The feel of his erection against her back making her wet.

"I...I'm sorry, Master."

"Wasn't I good to you? Didn't I let you come?"

"Yes, Master."

"You take that for granted, don't you?" He spun her around, raising her hands over her head.

"No, Master. I know you were kind to me and took your time." Not all men cared if their partner enjoyed sex, but they should because the more she fucked Nick the more she wanted to fuck him in any way he desired because she always came and it was always mind blowing.

He laughed. "You have no idea what I'm talking about." He moved closer, holding her in place with his body—large and strong against her. "Same safeword, right?"

She nodded. He wouldn't hurt her. This was a game.

"Don't lower your arm." He let go of one of her wrists and moved the other to the right. He reached up with his other hand, all the while keeping his eyes locked with hers. His were dark and intense and filled with excitement.

His nearness and the desire in his gaze made her inhale which caused her breasts to rub against his chest. His nostrils flared and she couldn't stop a soft sigh from slipping past her lips. The friction on her already hard nipples was wonderful. There was a click and he grabbed her other hand. She gazed upward, something was around her wrist, holding it in place. It was soft but firm.

"Nick, I mean, Master?" She was cuffed to the door.

He latched the other wrist far to the left and then bent, grabbing her ankle and pulling it to the left. He strapped a cuff around it, latching it in place and did the same for her other leg. She was spread out in an X on the door, her thighs open wide for him. She tugged on her restraints but they didn't give. She was helpless and his. Her panties got wetter and her nipples harder.

He stepped back and turned on the light. He looked delicious in a pair of jeans and T-shirt. His dark eyes were hot with desire and his erection already strained against his pants. He walked to the bar and poured himself a drink. He tossed it back and added more, bringing it to her and raising it to her lips. "Drink."

She didn't care for scotch but tonight she had no choice—she glanced down at her legs spread wide—in a lot of things. She swallowed the alcohol until he pulled the glass away. He refilled it again, this time adding ice, and stood in front of her, studying her. "You're overdressed. Don't you think?"

"Yes, Master." She did. She really did. She

wanted to be naked like this. She wanted him to fuck her against the door with her at his mercy, unable to move.

He pulled a key from his pocket and unlatched one of her hands. "Take off your shirt."

It was a T-shirt, tight across her breasts. She out of one side and then pulled it over her head. It hung, still affixed on her other arm. He moved closer, pressing her back against the door with his body. He reached around her, unclasping her bra and letting it gape forward. His eyes locked on her breasts, her nipples tight little buds waiting for his hand or mouth, hopefully both.

He pulled the bra off her free arm and re-latched her wrist. He unlocked the other but didn't let her lower it. He shoved the shirt and bra up and off her arm before hooking her back into the restraint. He pulled an ice cube from his drink and popped it into his mouth. He lowered his head, his lips surrounding her nipple. The heat from his mouth warred with the coldness of the ice and she moaned, arching forward. Her arms struggled in the restraints, wanting to pull him closer, run her fingers through his hair as he sucked her tit, but she couldn't move. Instead, she wriggled, rubbing herself against his erection. She needed him to touch her there, between her legs.

"No, my dear, not yet." He shifted his hips away from her. "You haven't been punished nearly enough." He popped another piece of ice in his mouth and kissed her neck, finding the spot that seemed to be directly linked to her pussy.

"Oh, god. Please, Ni...Master. I'll be good. Please."

"I don't believe you." His mouth found her nipple

again and his hand trailed downward. He unbuttoned her jeans and unzipped them.

She tried to hold still, hoping he'd touch her, but his lips were working her breast, making her body writhe in ecstasy. Then, he stepped away, leaving her aching. His eyes were black with desire as he dropped to his knees. She closed her eyes, saying a silent prayer of gratitude. He unhooked her ankles and yanked down her pants and underwear. He stared at her pussy, the wetness running down her thighs. "You're close aren't you."

"Yes. Yes, Master."

He trailed a finger up her thigh and her legs quivered as he got closer and closer. She couldn't take her eyes from his hand, his finger. She wiggled her hips, trying to urge him to move faster. She almost cried when he dropped his hand and stood.

"Do exactly as I say or I won't let you come at all tonight," he whispered in her ear.

She nodded, starting to realize he didn't mean he'd fuck her badly, but torture her by bringing her close to release but never taking her over the edge.

He unhooked her wrists. "Turn around."

She spun around. He was going to fuck her from behind. It was one of her favorite positions.

"Raise your arms."

She did.

He snapped the cuffs around her wrists. "Spread your legs for me."

She did. Gladly. Eagerly. If he didn't hurry she was going to drip all over the floor she was so ready for him.

She felt his hair against her ass as he bent and latched her legs in the restraints.

"Stare at the door. Don't try and look at me."

She faced the door. She heard something hit the floor, like cloth. She clenched her inner muscles trying to get some relief. He was undressing. He'd fuck her soon. There was the sound of his zipper and then him stepping out of his pants. He moved closer, she could feel the heat of his body against her back. His erection, hot and hard, was against her ass. She was breathing heavy. If she could move, she'd press back against him. She wanted to beg but she didn't think that'd do anything but make him delay.

"I was without you for a week because you ran away." He moved closer until his entire body was pressed against hers. "Do you know what that does to a man?"

She shook her head.

He grabbed her hair in his fist and yanked a little – not enough to hurt, but enough to make her pay attention. "Answer me."

"No, Master."

"It does this." He thrust his dick against her. "I've had a hard on for days. My only relief my hand. Do you think that's fair? I paid for you. You were to fuck me whenever and however I wanted but instead you ran away. You left me to fuck myself."

"I…I'm sorry, Master."

"Not sorry enough." He let go of her hair and moved it aside. He kissed her neck until she squirmed. "The problem is, I want you too much to teach you a real lesson." His hands trailed down her back, one of them slipping around to her front, lightly gliding over her mound, just enough to tease.

She wanted to exclaim hallelujah but that'd be a mistake.

"But no matter how much I want you, I'm not ready to let you come. You're going to be begging me, weeping even before I'm done with you."

His words made the breath catch in her throat. He was too hard, too close to his release to play too long and she wasn't in the position to suck him off.

His hand moved upward, capturing her breast as he positioned himself between her butt cheeks. "I should fuck your ass, but you need to be relaxed the first time." He kissed her ear. "Later though." He slapped her butt and started rocking between her cheeks. He pushed her ass together and thrust, his movement rubbing her pussy against the door. She moaned and twisted. She was so close.

"Oh, no you don't." He reached around, grabbing her hips and keeping his arm between her and the door. "I'm going to be inside you when you come."

"Yes. Please, Nick." That's what she wanted. Him inside of her.

He shifted and thrust his penis between her thighs and along her cunt. "You're so wet." He lowered his face to her neck, breathing heavy. "Fuck this. I don't want to hotdog you."

He shoved inside of her and she threw back her head, moaning. This is what she'd wanted, needed. She turned her face and kissed his neck. He rammed into her again and again.

"Don't...you...come." His fingers dug into her

hips as he thrust again.

She was so close. She pushed back as he thrust forward. "Nick." He shifted, changing his angle and taking her away from the precipice of her orgasm. 'No, please. Like before."

"No." His word was guttural and his dick was growing and getting harder inside of her.

"No, wait," she begged. He was going to come without her.

And he did. He shoved into her hard and moaned as he arched against her, his cock twitching inside of her. He kissed her shoulder and pulled out. He slapped her ass. "That was a good girl. You didn't come, but you did look at me."

She was trembling, she'd been so close and he'd left her unfulfilled. There was the sound of his zipper. He was getting dressed. She prayed he was going to get on his knees or at least use his hands. Something, anything to relieve this tension, this pressure inside of her.

He walked away and when he came back he put a mask over her face, blinding her. "Do exactly what I say, or remember, I won't let you come at all tonight."

"Please."

"Please what?" He unhooked her ankles.

"Please, I need to come…Master."

"And you will. Several times."

Her knees buckled. Several times would be good, very good.

"But only if you're a good girl and do exactly what I say." He pinched her nipple and she gasped. "You already disobeyed by looking at me. Kissing me. Trying to coax me into letting you come."

"I...I'm sorry Master."

"Now, you'll have to wear the blindfold. Do you agree that's a fitting punishment?"

"Yes, Master." Not being able to see him was turning her on even more and although that was dangerous because she might combust, it was also hot.

He unlocked her hands. "Turn around."

She did and he fastened the restraints again.

"Now, we'll see how well you obey."

She heard more ice clink into his glass and more scotch being poured. He held the glass to her lips and she drank, coughing a bit. Her nipples, hardened even more, hoping for more ice and his mouth, but his body heat moved away from her chest. He was on his knees. Her juices flowed thick and lush, drenching her thighs in anticipation.

"Don't make a sound." A moment later, his hot mouth was on her, his tongue pushing the ice against her swollen flesh.

She couldn't help it. She screamed. He pulled his face way from her pussy and she whimpered at the loss.

"Do I have to gag you?"

"No! No, Master." The blindfold was a turn on but she had no desire for one of those ball gags. The only thing she wanted in her mouth was his dick or his tongue.

"Don't make a sound. Nothing. Do you understand?"

She started to speak but stopped and nodded her head.

"Good." He slapped her thigh, hard.

She clamped her teeth together to keep from moaning.

"That's my girl."

The ice clinked in his glass and his tongue trailed up her slit, rough and strong. She bit her lip as he circled her clit. He moved away and she wanted to beg but his mouth came down on her, sucking as he rubbed a piece of ice over her pussy lips and clit. She gasped, but managed to silence her moan although her body trembled and she thrust toward him. He grabbed her hips, holding her still as his tongue danced around her labia and then flicked her clit. This time, she couldn't contain the moan. He shook his head, giving her one last, long lick before standing. "I expected more from you."

She was panting. She needed him to finish her off. "Please Master."

He grabbed her face and kissed her. She tasted her own musk on his face and tongue. He was right. His face was full of her juices and it wasn't humiliating at all. It was turning her on. He was hers. The most intimate part of her was marking his handsome face.

He stepped away, his footsteps moving toward the couch. She strained and picked up the sound of him sitting and then drinking. She trembled, wanting to call him back to her but afraid he'd either refuse or gag her.

He stood and moved toward her but hesitated a few feet from her. There was the soft whisper of cloth against skin before he approached. Her heart raced, waiting for his touch. She could smell his cologne and feel the heat from his body but he didn't touch her. Her nerves were on fire, wanting him to stop this torture and then his hand brushed

over her hip and there was the click of the door. She
started moving forward. He'd opened the door!

"N…Master, where are you going?"

"That's not your place to ask." He slapped her
thigh with something and it stung, but it wasn't his hand. A
whip of some sort, long and thin. "Apologize."

"I'm sorry, Master."

"That's better." His hand caressed her breast and
trailed down her stomach. "Now, be a good girl while I'm
gone." His fingers dipped inside her and there was
something else—hard and circular. "Don't let the egg
drop." His lips brushed against her ear. "You're so tight,
that shouldn't be a problem."

She clenched her inner muscles, clamping down on
the object as he moved his hand and stepped into the
hallway, closing the door behind him. He'd be back in a
minute. He had to be. This was only part of the game.

CHAPTER 2: SARAH

Sarah strained to hear any sound but there was nothing. The minutes ticked by. Blind and strung up, a few moments felt like hours. Nick wouldn't leave her like this. He wouldn't. But if something happened to him, she'd be stuck here, naked and bound. The maids would find her in the morning but what if he put the Do Not Disturb sign on the door? She could scream but oh God, she didn't want to be discovered like this. Her heart raced and her face heated. She should've never let him do this to her. Yes, it'd been hot and if she were honest, it still was but if he didn't come back...

Suddenly, there was a jolt from the device she clutched inside of her. It sent a wave of shock and pleasure, deep, penetrating pleasure through her. She tightened her grip, trying to squeeze her legs shut to apply more pressure but she couldn't move. The vibrations stopped and she waited, in darkness anticipating the pleasure and then it went off again. One tiny jolt that she felt to her toes. Her nipples tightened again and she clasped down hard with her inner muscles, hoping that'd trigger the vibrator to send its jolt again but there was nothing.

Her mind danced between worrying about being left there and waiting for the vibrator to start again. The jolt happened again but this time it wasn't only one, quick vibration. The little toy hummed, sending wave after wave of sensation through her. She tried to squirm but couldn't move. She moaned and the door opened, swinging her forward and someone came inside and closed the door. She prayed it was Nick.

"Do you like that?" Nick's voice whispered in her ear as his fingers pinched her nipples. "I thought you would."

"Yes, please."

"Please what?" He pinched her nipple again and her gasp turned into a moan as the vibrations inside her increased tempo.

"Please, Master."

"Are you ready to come?" His hand cupped her mound, his fingers dipping inside her. "Fuck, you're so wet."

"Yes, I need to come. Please."

"No." He removed his hand and turned off the vibrator. He pulled off her mask and went to the couch and sat. His dick was hard again by the bulge in his pants.

"Please, Master. I'll be good. I won't run away. I swear." If she didn't come soon, she'd die. It was that simple.

His dark eyes raked over her. "I think you've experience a little of the frustration I felt when you weren't here. Hot, horny and alone isn't any fun. Is it?"

"No." She wasn't sure he was still talking about this fantasy.

"What do you do when you're alone? Do you find another lover?"

"No." She was pretty sure this wasn't about the game.

He walked over to her, his chest pressing her back against the door. "Then what do you do?" He rubbed his cock against her pussy. "When you're ready to come?" He touched her lips, stopping her from answering. "I want the truth, Sarah."

"I take care of it myself." Embarrassment flooded her face and chest.

"Vibrator, dildo, fingers or something else." His black eyes sparkled with heat.

She locked eyes with his. She had no reason to be embarrassed about this. "All of the above."

He strode over to the bar. Poured her a drink of Crown Royale and brought it back to her. "Drink up."

She gulped the alcohol until he moved it from her lips. He went back to the bar, poured himself a drink and began digging around in a case that he must've put there when she was blindfolded. He placed his drink on the coffee table and came back to her.

He unlatched her right hand. "Show me." He held out a vibrator and a dildo.

The breath froze in her chest as she stared at his offerings. Her eyes shot to his. He wasn't kidding.

"Choose or I choose for you."

She took the vibrator and he grabbed a chair, moving it a few feet from her.

"Anytime." He snatched his glass from the table and relaxed against the seat, taking a sip of his drink, his dark eyes never leaving her.

There was a warning in his tone. If she didn't obey, he'd punish her again and she really needed release. She pressed a button and the vibrator hummed to life. The sound making her juices start to flow again and her nipples tighten. She'd get to come and it'd be quick.

"Look at me," his voice was thick with desire.

She raised her gaze to his. He unzipped his pants, his dick already standing at attention.

"I'm waiting." His hand was hovering over his cock.

She lowered the vibrator to her pussy and gasped at the initial feel – so good. She closed her eyes.

"Look at me, Sarah!"

She opened her eyes and he was stroking himself in long, strong strokes. She rubbed the vibrator up and down one side, searching for the spot that she liked although different days made for different motions and places. She moaned as she hit a very sensitive place and circled her clit.

"That's it." He stroked faster.

She kept rubbing the vibrator along her wet pussy, as she watched his dick lengthen and his face harden with passion. They were both close and then he stood, striding over to her and taking the vibrator from her hands.

"I'm going to finish you off." He rubbed it along her clit as his mouth came down hard on her breast, sucking and nipping and then his fingers were inside her as the vibrator worked her clit.

Her muscles clenched around his fingers and she screamed. "Oh...oh Nick. Yes."

He kept thrusting his fingers inside her and rubbing the vibrator along her cunt, prolonging her orgasm. She collapsed, held up only by the restraints. She didn't have a working muscle or bone in her body. They'd all liquefied and flowed out her pussy and down her legs.

"Again," he said, as he pushed his cock into her.

She gasped as he rotated his hips and thrust, finding her g-spot.

"Nick. I can't. Please." Her free hand tangled in his hair, finally able to touch him.

"You can and you will."

"Please. I can't." She'd never survive another orgasm. "Not yet."

"Use the safeword if you need it." When she didn't say anything, he grabbed her hand and re-cuffed her as he kissed her, his tongue matching the pumping of the lower part of his body and soon she was kissing him back, her hips working with his rhythm.

"Please, I want to touch you."

"No." He nipped her neck. "Master."

"Please, Master."

"No." He moved his mouth to her breast and his hand to her pussy, searching until he found her hard little nub. He flicked it in time with his thrusts and she closed her eyes, riding the wave of passion he created inside her. But soon, her body tensed and tightened.

"Harder, Master. Harder."

He increased his tempo, slamming her against the door and she broke apart—shattered, the inner muscles grasping him and he moaned against her neck and shuddered his release.

After several moments he bent, unhooking her ankles. Her knees buckled and he used his body to hold her up. He unlatched her hands and carried her to the bedroom. He placed her under the covers and crawled in next to her, pulling her close.

He kissed the top of her head. "You okay."

"Better than okay." She smiled against his chest.

His hand trailed up and down her back. "I have to ask. How did you ever come up with cat litter as your safeword? I about burst out laughing when I saw it last week."

"I wanted something I could use every time and I wanted something that I didn't think we'd use in any of our fantasies."

"And cat litter was all you could come up with?" His tone was amused.

"Exactly. I thought flower but…" her face heated a bit. "A woman's…vagina is sometime referred to as her flower. Then I thought of different fruit but what if you decide to feed me during one of the games."

"Very thorough and you're right. I don't think I have any sexual scenarios where I'd say or use cat litter."

CHAPTER 3: SARAH

Sarah shifted out from under Nick's arm and crawled out of the bed.

"Where are you going?" he mumbled.

"I have to leave." She didn't want to. He was all rumpled, his cheeks bristly. She wanted to crawl back into that bed and never leave.

He rolled over, the covers tenting over his arousal. "Stay. Just for a bit." He patted the bed. "Please."

It was getting harder and harder for her to deny him anything. "You have to make it fast."

"I can do that." He grinned as he lifted the covers.

She crawled back into the bed, sinking into the mattress and against his body.

His mouth came down on hers, his lips soft and coaxing as he leaned over her. Her hands trailed up his back as her leg skimmed across his, opening so he could move into position.

"You're wet already," he said against her ear.

"Always for you." It was true. The thought of him made her body soften, waiting for him to be inside her.

He leaned up, staring at her and there was something besides desire in his eyes. It made her nervous.

"Say that again." He clasped her head between his hands.

"I'm always wet for you."

"Fuck, that's hot." His mouth came down on hers, his tongue thrusting inside as he shifted so he was between her thighs. His dick pressed against her thigh and she opened wider for him. "I need you now."

"Yes." She needed him now too.

"Only you and me. Nothing else. Nothing between us." He whispered in her ear. His fingers stroking her. "Say, it Sarah."

"Yes, Nick. Only you and me." She had no idea why he needed her to say that, but right now she didn't care.

He thrust inside her and she gasped, he was so hot and slick. Her hands wrapped around his neck as her hips rocked with his rhythm. This felt so good, so right and then she froze.

"Condom. You didn't put on a condom."

He thrust again. "You feel so good, baby. Just me and you."

"Nick. You need to put on a condom." She grabbed his hair and yanked.

"Please." He kissed her ear. "You feel so good like this. You agreed."

"I didn't agree. I didn't know what you were

talking about." She shoved his chest as she tried to squirm away.

"No, baby. Please don't make me stop." He kissed her neck as he kept fucking her. "You don't know how good you feel."

"Stop! Stop, now." She thrashed under him, but he was too big. She couldn't get away. Tears rolled down her cheeks. This couldn't be happening.

He pulled out of her and rolled away. "Damnit, Sarah. You said okay." He sat up, furious.

She climbed out of bed, yanking the sheet with her and covering herself. "I didn't know what you meant. I'd never agree to that. Never."

"What's the big, fucking deal. One time. You said we could talk about it and you agreed. Only you and me, nothing between us. What did you think I was talking about?"

"What's the big deal?" Her heart slammed against her chest. He didn't understand. He was a man, how could he?

"Yeah. I haven't had anyone, *anyone* since you. I'm clean and you're on birth control so what's the big, fucking deal."

A muscle twitched in his cheek, he was furious but so was she. Furious and scared. Petrified.

"You...you want to know what the big deal is?" Her words poured from her. Words that she'd never meant to say, ever, to anyone. "A baby. That's what. We'll do this and I'll get pregnant and you'll leave me for Lisa and...and I'll be alone and terrified and then you'll die and..." She gasped for breath. She'd said too much. He was staring at her, confused and with pity. Oh, she couldn't take the pity.

She ran toward the other room and the door. All she needed was her purse. She'd flee in the sheet. She didn't care. Nothing was as important as getting out of there.

"Sarah, wait!"

She'd made it halfway through the living room before Nick's arm wrapped around her waist, lifting her off her feet.

"Let me go." She kicked at him and elbowed him in the gut but he only grunted and tightened his hold.

"Calm down."

"Cat litter. Cat litter. Let me go."

He sat on the couch, pulling her onto his lap and holding her close. "That only works when we're playing and we're definitely not playing."

"Please. Let me go." In a minute, she was going to breakdown and she needed to be alone when that happened.

"No. Never." He kissed the top of her head and she burst into tears.

She buried her face against his chest and cried. She cried for Adam and their baby and the life none of them would ever have. It was several minutes later when she realized Nick was saying soothing words, calling her baby and love, but he didn't mean it. He was just a good guy. She shifted away from him and dried her eyes on the sheet.

"Better." He ducked his head so he could see her face.

She nodded. "I do have to go."

"Not until you tell me what happened." His arm

tightened around her, pulling her close to him again.

"No. It's person—"

"Enough." He swatted her bottom but not hard. "We've long since passed Ethan's rules."

She did kind of owe him an explanation. She'd had a breakdown while they were having sex. Plus, she'd already said most of it.

"I'll ask you questions if that makes it easier." He brushed the hair away from her face. "Who's Lisa?"

"She's the other girl. The one Adam fell in love with. Remember?" She inhaled deeply. That wasn't so hard.

"Adam was a fool." He kissed her head again and she smiled and kissed his chest.

"Was Adam the father?"

She nodded, her breathing becoming shallow. She didn't want to talk about the baby.

"What happened to him?"

"He died." Tears trickled down her cheeks. "He was in the service. He...got caught in gunfire."

"Shit. I'm sorry." His arms tightened around her. "I mean, I hate the son-of-a-bitch, but I'm sorry he's dead."

"He was a good guy."

"He abandoned you when you were pregnant."

"No." She sat up so she could see him. His mouth was drawn in a tight line. "I never told him."

"What? Why?"

"I...I was going to. He called and I was so excited." She trembled, remembering that day. It was the third worst in her life. "I couldn't wait to tell him about the baby but he wanted to talk first. He said he was in love with Lisa and they were getting married." She took a deep breath. "I was such a fool. They'd broken up a week or so after the party and we'd gotten back together before he deployed again. I thought he loved me."

"He was an idiot." He kissed her softly.

"I...I didn't know what to say. What to do. He said that us being together that last time had been a mistake." She touched her stomach. "A mistake. Our baby was a mistake. That's all I could think."

"Oh, sweetheart. I'm so sorry."

"I didn't want it. I wanted it gone. I wanted all part of him, any reminder of him, gone." She looked up at Nick. He'd hate her when she admitted this. "That's why the baby died. She knew she wasn't wanted. She wasn't loved." She burst into tears again. She was a horrible person to hate an innocent baby, her baby.

"Miscarriages happen. They're horrible and tragic but they happen." He stroked her hair.

"But, I didn't want the baby and then Adam died and...then the baby died and it was the last part of him and...and I destroyed it."

He pulled her even closer. "It wasn't your fault. None of this."

"But I didn't want my baby."

He grabbed her face and made her look at him. "But that's not why your baby died." He shook her gently. "And that's not why Adam died."

"I...I know but...it still feels like my fault. My failure."

"Stop." He kissed her again. "You didn't fail anyone." He pulled her to his chest. "You need to listen to me. It was a bad thing that happened…two bad things but none of it is your fault. None of it."

She buried her face in his chest, hoping one day she could believe him.

Book 6

The Proposition

CHAPTER 1: SARAH

Sarah hurried to the door and opened it.

"Wow! You look great." Lisa stepped into the house and bent to pet Tank.

"Thanks." Her hand skimmed over the silky, green dress. She'd bought this for Nick.

"Must be some project." Lisa glanced up at her.

"I..." Her words froze. Lisa had seen her dressed up on several occasions. The other woman had to suspect that Sarah wasn't working.

"Listen." Lisa stood, her hand still resting on Tank's head. "I'm glad for you."

"Oh. You are?"

"Yeah." Lisa smiled. "I'm glad you found someone."

"What? I didn't." She hadn't. Nick wasn't someone, not like Lisa meant.

"Oh. I'm sorry. It's only that you…The way you've been dressing and how late it is when you come home." Lisa glanced down at Tank. "And how rumpled you are when you get here. I thought you'd met someone."

"Well, I didn't." She moved toward the door, but Lisa didn't step aside. "Excuse me."

Lisa still didn't move and she wasn't going to get into a fight. So, she took a deep breath. She didn't want to have this conversation. It was bad enough when she had similar ones with her family but it appeared that Lisa wanted to have her say, so the fastest way to get out of there was to listen and leave.

"Say it. You might as well. It won't change how I feel about you." She almost cringed as the last words slipped through her lips. She needed to control her mouth when she lost her temper.

"No, I suppose it won't." There was a weariness to Lisa's tone. "I just think that getting out and meeting…people would be good for Tank…and you."

"I am getting out." She tipped her head. "Thanks to you." She meant that. She really did.

"Tom told me to keep my mouth shut about this, but I can't." Lisa took a deep breath. "I'm sorry Adam and I hurt you."

"You've apologized before. I understand. You didn't mean to fall in love. It just happened." That was a bullshit reason for Adam to cheat on her. They'd been together for years.

"Yes, we did and…I'm sorry but you shouldn't be

hiding away like this."

"I'm not hiding. I'm taking care of Tank."

"Yes, but you're also hiding. Adam died not you."

"Don't." She backed away and Tank started pacing and whining.

"I'm sorry but it's true. You stopped living when Adam died." Lisa stepped closer to her.

"I did not. I built a business. I've helped countless animals and people."

"But you haven't put yourself out there. Allowed yourself to meet a man and...to fall in love again."

She shook her head. "I've been busy. It's not that simple."

"No, it's not. It's hard to move on, to try again and it's scary." Lisa took her hand. "But Adam wouldn't want you to live like this. He still cared for you."

But not enough. Her heart raced in her chest. She needed to get out of there. "I've got to go." She shoved past Lisa and almost ran out the door.

CHAPTER 2: NICK

Nick checked his watch. Sarah should be here in another five minutes or so, unless she was late. She'd better not be late. He poured them each a drink and started the radio on his phone. He picked a station that played slow, romantic songs and took his drink and sat on the couch. He hated waiting. Usually, people waited on him, but not Sarah. She'd never treated him like everyone else. He grinned as he sipped his scotch. That's part of what he liked about her. She didn't care that he was rich. Of course, she had no idea how rich he was.

The card clicked in the door and it opened. She looked amazing in an emerald green dress with her hair piled on her head in some kind of style that left tendrils escaping down her long neck. He wanted to follow those little wisps of hair with his lips and tongue, but not now. Later. He'd definitely do that later.

"Hello." He stood and went and retrieved her drink,

taking it to her.

She was gazing around the room a soft smile on her face. "Thank you."

She took the drink, but he was pretty sure the thanks was for the room. It did look amazing. There were flowers of every kind the florist could think of in vases around the room. There was champagne and strawberries on the table and the lights were low.

"The food will be here soon. I ordered an early dinner." He held out his hand. "Would you like to dance?"

She took a sip of her drink and placed it on a nearby table. Then she took his hand, and he set his drink next to hers and led her to a clear area in the living room. He pulled her close and began to dance, amazed at how perfect she felt in his arms, against his body.

She rested her head on his shoulder, the soft perfume of her hair turning him on. How many mornings had he buried his head in her pillow inhaling her scent? Well, five actually and that wasn't enough, but he'd get more.

CHAPTER 3: SARAH

Sarah almost melted against him. He was so sweet and this was so wonderful she almost cried. She didn't want their time together to end, but it would. It had to. His warm breath tickled her neck as he breathed in the scent of her hair. One of his hands held hers and the other rested on the small of her back. She wanted it lower. This romance was nice, lovely even but she wanted him. She shifted a little closer, brushing against his erection.

He kissed her neck softly. When he didn't do anything else she did it again.

"Keep doing that and we'll be naked before dinner," he rumbled against her ear.

"So." She tipped her head so she could see him.

His hands pulled her hips closer and he rocked against her. "Sarah, I thought we should wait until…"

She stepped away, keeping a hold of his hand and leading him to the couch. She shoved his chest and he sat, his black eyes hungry as they roamed over her, making her panties wet.

"I thought tonight was my night to decide what we do?" His voice was raspy with desire. He was enjoying this as much as she was.

"It is." She knelt in front of him, shoving his legs apart and skimming her fingers up his thighs. "If I do anything." Her fingers trailed across his erection. "Anything." She undid his button. "That you don't want me to do." She unzipped his pants and he lifted, so she could pull them down. "Tell me." She took his engorged penis in her hand. "And I'll stop." Her eyes locked with his as she lowered her mouth toward his cock. "Should I continue?" She let her warm breath brush over him.

"Yes." His voice was thick with desire.

She loved the feel of him in her hand, smooth and hard and hot, so hot. She licked the top of his penis, lapping up his pre-cum. It was salty and musky. She did it again, letting her tongue caress the engorged head. He moaned and she almost smiled. He was hers now and she loved the taste and scent of him. She licked around the top as her hands worked up and down his length.

"Sarah, please." His hand touched her head, guiding her down and she took him in, sucking the tip.

"Oh, fuck, that feels so good." His fingers wrapped in her hair as he thrust upward into her mouth.

She cupped his balls and squeezed a little while she sucked him deeper into her mouth. He thrust upward, hitting the back of her throat and she struggled not to gag. She didn't want to ruin this for him. She worked her tongue on the tip as she continued the suction. His balls were tight and his dick was twitching. He was going to come soon.

"Sa..rah." He tapped her on the shoulder, signaling for her to stop.

She worked her hand faster on his length while she sucked harder.

"Fuck, I'm coming." His eyes locked with hers.

His cock seemed to get longer and harder before hot jets of cum filled her mouth. She kept sucking, swallowing as much as she could as he kept spurting and then his body eased and she slid her mouth off his penis, licking the tip to clean him. The taste wasn't bad. She wouldn't order it for dessert but she'd do this again for him. She sobered at the thought. No. She probably wouldn't.

"Are you okay?" He asked, watching her.

She smiled. "Yeah." She went and got their drinks, wiping her face on a napkin from the bar before going back to the couch and sitting next to him.

He'd put his dick back in his pants and he pulled her onto his lap. "You didn't have to—"

"I know, but I wanted to."

He kissed her. It was a warm kiss, promising passion later. "

"Was it your first time?"

She glanced away. "You could tell?"

He turned her head toward him. "It was great." He kissed her again.

"Then how did you know?" She must've shown her inexperience. She'd given blow jobs before, to him before, but she'd never swallowed. She'd never wanted to and Adam had never asked. Their sex life hadn't been like that.

Like this, with Nick.

"Your face. Afterwards." He tried not to grin.

"Probably when I came too but I was a bit preoccupied."

"Was it that bad?" she asked.

"No." He gave up and laughed. "You looked really, really surprised and...puzzled."

"Stop laughing at me." She slapped his chest playfully. "I was a bit surprised."

"By what?" He was trying not to laugh but continued to fail miserably.

"Well..." Her face heated, but this was Nick. There were no secrets with him. Not in this hotel room. Not about sex. Everything else was a secret but nothing that had to do with their nights together. "I was a bit surprised by the quantity and the heat and the...velocity."

He burst out laughing and she slapped him again.

"It's not funny. You'd be surprised too."

"By a guy coming in my mouth? Hell yeah, I'd be surprised and then he'd be dead."

"You know what I meant."

"I do.' He tossed back his drink and put it on the table next to the couch. "We'll make sure to practice that more so you're not so surprised next time." He kissed her.

"So, you liked it?"

"Fuck, yeah." He kissed her again as his hand wandered up her dress. "But now, it's time for you to work up an appetite." He laid her on the couch, his hands skimming up her thighs taking her dress with them.

She relaxed, waiting as his mouth kissed its way upward—open, wet and hot. His finger pressed against her pussy, rubbing and she squirmed, all relaxation gone as tension began to build.

"Green. Lovely." He tugged on her underwear, slipping his finger inside the leg hole as his mouth came down on her mound, kissing and nibbling.

She squirmed again, pushing closer to him. This was great but it wasn't enough. She wanted his mouth on her, not her panties. "Please, Nick." She reached down, pushing at her underwear to remove it, but he grabbed her hands.

"Not yet." He pulled them away from her leg, his tongue darting underneath where his finger had been, tickling her with his quick caress.

Her panties were soaked from his mouth and her moisture, and getting wetter as his hand caressed her little bud and his tongue jabbed at her inner lips.

He moved away, yanking her underwear down and off her legs and then he was back, his tongue lapping at her. She thrust toward him, wanting him more, deeper, harder. He lifted her legs, placing them over his shoulders and his hands grasped her ass, lifting her off the couch as he feasted on her. She moaned, long past words as he lapped and suckled, his tongue rough as it teased her nub. Then his fingers were inside of her, thrusting and her body coiled tighter and tighter. She wanted to move, to race to meet her climax but his grip was firm, holding her in place. His mouth came down on her clit and he sucked.

"Oh....oh..." She was so close.

He stopped, holding her still, his face brushing against her thigh as he turned his head.

"Oh God, Nick, please don't stop."

He pulled her legs down, bending them at the knees.

"Dinner's here."

She leaned up. "You're kidding?" He had to be kidding. He'd better be kidding.

He grinned at her as he stood. "Nope. They're at the door."

"Shit." She flopped back down. "One more minute. That's all I needed."

He tugged her dress down so it covered her thighs. "Stay here. I'll be right back."

"What?" She started to sit up, but he stopped her. "Stay."

"You can't be serious."

There was another knock.

"One minute," he called out as his eyes locked with hers. "I'm very serious. If you want me to pick this back up. You'll stay right like that." He turned and headed for the door.

She was splayed out on the couch, her legs open and bent at the knees. Anyone who saw her, and they would see her—the table was in the same room and only a few feet away—would know what they'd been doing...what they were going to be doing.

Nick opened the door and as he stepped aside she sat up. He motioned for the two young men to come inside.

"Shall we set the table for you?" asked the one man.

"Please." Nick glanced in her direction and his eyes narrowed when he saw her upright on the couch.

She walked over to the bar, her legs still rubbery from unspent passion and poured herself a drink. She'd come tonight, there was no doubt, but first he'd make her pay for disobeying him. She squeezed her thighs together in anticipation of the exquisite torture to come.

As soon as the table was set, Nick paid the men and they left. He closed the door and leaned against it, watching her.

"There was no way I was going to let them see me like that."

"Why? You looked beautiful. Better than beautiful. Sexy. Hot. Wanton. Desirable." He walked toward her. "Any man who saw you would've wanted you."

She finished her drink and strolled toward him. "Is that why you wanted me to stay like that?"

He stopped only inches from her. "Yes." He almost snarled. "I wanted them to know you're mine."

She wrapped her arms around his neck. This was their last night and he was being possessive. It made her heart ache. "I think me being in here is proof enough of that."

"Proof. But not enough." He kissed her, grabbing her ass and lifting her off the ground as he pressed her against him.

He was hard again and she wiggled her hips. This was way better than his tongue. He set her on the bar. He shoved her skirt up and she spread her legs, making room for him, but he stepped away.

"Stay right there." He grabbed her chin. "I mean it." He kissed her and went into the bedroom. He came back a moment later and stopped in front of her, staring at the place between her legs. "Open for me."

She spread her legs wider. Eager to obey.

"No, your lips." He motioned between her legs.

"Pull them apart. I want to see you."

She flushed but did as he asked. She was on display and his eyes were making her wet and ready for him. The bulge in his pants was getting bigger. He stepped forward, his fingers caressing up and down her vagina. One of them dipped inside and she moaned. He kissed her, hard and dominant. She wrapped her arms and legs around him and his hand moved from her pussy to her breast, but his other hand replaced the first and then he was putting something inside her.

She broke the kiss. "Nick…what?"

He stopped her hand from reaching between her legs. "Leave it." He kissed her fingers. "It's the egg, remember."

Her inner muscles clamped down around the little vibrator. "Yes."

"Let's eat." He took her hand, his eyes sparkling with desire and a promise that dinner was going to be unforgettable. He helped her off the bar. He kept her hand in his as he led her to the table, only letting go to hold her chair as she sat. He took the seat across from her and she waited for him to start the egg but he motioned at her plate.

"Aren't you hungry?" He ate a piece of the bread and cut into his lasagna.

"It smells delicious." She took a bite. "It's good." It was excellent lasagna. The best she'd ever had, but she couldn't concentrate on the food with the silent vibrator inside of her.

He began chatting about television and a little about his work, without going into any details and the entire time, she thought about the egg. When was he going to start it?

How long would he let it vibrate? How long before he let her come?

He put is fork down. "Is something wrong?" The smug look on his face belied his tone of concern.

"Damnit, Nick. Give me the control." She held out her hand.

"What? This?" He pulled a small device from his pocket and pressed a button.

She straightened, her hand dropping to the table, as vibrations shot through her pussy and then stopped. "Please, Nick."

"Please, what? More?"

The egg started again and she closed her eyes, squeezing her legs together. That little toy felt so good and she was already so close.

"Look at me."

She opened her eyes. His were dark and his face was hard with desire. He put the control on the table by his plate so she could see everything he did and then he pushed another button. The vibrations of the egg ramped up and she almost shot to her feet. It was too much. She tossed back her head and moaned, her mouth open and panting. It felt great and hot and almost painful. He moved around the table and lifted her, carrying her to the bedroom.

He put her on the bed, the vibrator continuing to send waves of pleasure through her. He undid his pants, bending her legs at the knees and spreading them wide. He grabbed the handled of the egg and removed it before pushing inside of her. She gasped, he was so hard and long, filling her. He thrust once and she tightened her legs around him, her feet on his ass, helping him to thrust deeper.

"Harder, please," she begged and he obeyed.

The bed rocked as he slammed into her and she broke apart her fingers clasping at his shoulders as she gasped and shook in her release. He continued to rock into her, extending her pleasure and then his back arched and he groaned as he came.

He flopped onto her, but she didn't feel his weight, only comfort. Her bones were melted, and his warmth and strength a blessing. Too soon he pulled out of her. He kicked off his pants and pulled off his shirt. He bent, removing her dress and then lifted her, placing her head on the pillows before climbing in next to her and pulling her close.

CHAPTER 4: SARAH

Sarah snuggled against Nick's chest, struggling to stay awake. This little time they had left was precious and she didn't want to waste one moment sleeping.

"I was thinking." His hand ran up and down her back.

"Hmm." Her fingers skimmed over his chest, trying to memorize the feel of him for later.

"We should talk to Ethan and extend our time together."

"What?" Her hand froze.

"I want more time with you."

She pulled away. She wanted that too, but she couldn't have it. Lisa had already made plans for her last two Saturdays before deployment. She sat up, covering herself with the sheet. "I'd like the two more weeks too, but I can't. I'm sorry."

"Not just two weeks. I want another contract. A

longer one." He took her hand and kissed her palm.

"Oh." She hadn't expected that. She hadn't expected any of this. She'd hoped for good sex but not these feelings. "I'm sorry. I can't."

"What? Why not?" He sat up, a look of incredulousness on his face.

"I...I can't." She'd told him so much about her past. She couldn't let him get any closer. It'd hurt that much more when he left, and he would.

"Stop hiding behind Ethan's bullshit rules." He grabbed her and pulled her under him. "I know you want more of this too."

His mouth came down on hers and she opened for him. Every part of her opened for him and it'd only been six nights. Another six and her heart would be open to him too.

He stopped kissing her, but stayed leaning over her, surrounding her, his strength making her weak. She touched his face, wanting nothing more than to stay there forever. The part of her that didn't want to cry almost laughed. He'd probably never been turned down in his life. She kissed him. She had to make this rejection easy on him.

"I think, it'd be better for me if we both left wanting more." She kissed him again. "I do want more, but—"

"Then it's settled. We'll talk to Ethan. I understand you can only meet on Saturdays and an hour during the week. So, we should settle on another twenty-four nights."

"Six months?" That was a lot. She could never do that. Not that she was considering doing any more time, but she wanted to. She really wanted to, but that'd guarantee heartbreak for her and she'd had enough heartbreak for one lifetime. Plus, she had no one to watch Tank.

"Yeah." He kissed her. It was hot and erotica and persuasive.

She pulled away. "Nick, I can't."

"Why?" He brushed the hair from her face.

"You only want more time because you can't have it."

"That's not true. I want more time with you because I can't imagine not having you again."

She shook her head. "I can't." Her hand drifted down his chest toward his semi-aroused cock.

He stopped her before she could touch him and her heart sunk. He was going to ruin their last night together.

"You don't understand." He kissed her hand and placed it back on his chest. "If you want more than sixth months, that's fine."

"What are you saying?" Her body tensed, waiting for the pain because there was pain coming.

"According to our contract, we can see each other outside of La Petite Mort Club," he said.

"Only if we both contact Ethan in four months requesting the other person's contact information."

"Exactly." He kissed her, pressing her back to the bed.

"Four months, Nick."

He kissed her neck and shoulder. He tugged the blanket down, clearing his path to her breasts.

She grabbed his hair stopping him. "And what then?"

He used his leg to spread hers and positioned himself between her thighs, his erection lying on her stomach and pressing against her pussy which was already wet and hungry for him.

"Then we date like normal people." He grinned. "Not completely normal. I definitely want to play the professor again and I have some other toys that I think you'll enjoy or should I say, Sarah the Slave will enjoy."

A wave of lust washed over her. She wanted those things too but she couldn't have them. He wasn't the type to settle down with one woman and she wouldn't survive when he left her for someone else. Her mind scrambled to convince him that this was over, but without hurting him. She could never hurt him. "You'd have to be celibate for the four months. You could never do that."

He kissed her nose. "For you, I could."

That was it. Tears trickled from her eyes. He wasn't lying but it wasn't the truth either. He meant what he was saying but as soon as he had her for a few weeks, he'd grow tired of her.

"Don't cry, baby." He kissed her tears. "What's wrong?"

"You...you...don't mean it."

He grasped her face. "I do."

"I don't believe you. You said you grow tired of women after a month. A month!"

He sighed. "Not you."

She shook her head and cried harder. If only she could believe him. He rolled to the side, pulling her on top of him and stoking her hair.

"Don't cry, honey. I know I said that but that was

before I met you. It's different with you."

But it wasn't. He only thought it was because he couldn't have her when he wanted her. As soon as he did, it was over.

He kissed her head. "This is why Ethan has these time limits. Most people move on before four months and it saves…well, heartache and breakups."

"You'll move on." She said against his neck. She needed him to be honest with himself and with her.

His hands caressed her back again, dipping in the crack on her ass and pulling her against his erection. "I won't. I'll send a request to Ethan on day one-twenty at twelve-o-one."

He tipped her head up so she had to look at him and she wanted to believe him. He was so dear already and he truly believed what he was saying, the earnestness was all over his face.

"You do the same." He kissed her. It was gentle and coaxing. "I'll show you I'm serious about this. About us." His hand drifted lower between her ass cheeks, his fingers lightly skimming over her pussy.

She wanted him. This was their last night. She should tell him she wouldn't send the request to Ethan but then they'd fight and their last evening together would be ruined. She reached between their bodies and grabbed his cock. This was better. He'd never send the request either. This way they could finish the night in fantasy like they'd spent all their nights.

He moaned as she ran her thumb over the head of his dick. She squeezed harder and did it again.

"Suck me," he said.

She started kissing her way down his body but he grabbed her arm.

"Straddle my face. I want to eat you out while you suck my dick."

"Ah." Her pussy throbbed in anticipation but she didn't think she'd be able to concentrate enough to make it good for him.

"Do it." He swatted her ass. "Trust me." His eyes locked with hers, wanting her to trust him in this and more.

She moved up the bed. She'd trust him in this, but that was all. Her face heated a bit as she positioned herself over his face. He'd been there before but this was more embarrassing, more erotic, because it was like she was demanding he do this instead of accepting his attentions.

"That's it." His hand ran up her thighs, squeezing the cheeks of her ass. "Now, lower yourself."

She did, lowering her face to his dick and her pussy to his face. His fingers brushed against her curls as she licked his cock. He spread her lips and his tongue teased along her creases. She licked around his head, increasing her tempo with his.

"Put me in your mouth." His words vibrated against her pussy and she shivered.

She opened her mouth wide and took him inside, sucking gently. He flicked her clit and she moaned, making him groan. She sucked harder as his tongue darted inside her and then tapped her nub again. She moaned again and he thrust up into her mouth. She caressed his balls and he flicked her again. She was so close to coming, her hips pressed down toward him but he lifted her away and sat up.

Her heart raced. She wanted his cock in her mouth
and his tongue in her pussy but he grabbed her around the
waist and pulled her onto his lap.

"Get a condom and put it on me."

His fingers played in her curls, keeping her on the
edge as she grabbed a condom from the nightstand and
opened it, sliding it down his thick shaft.

"Put me inside you." He whispered against her ear.

She rubbed his length against her as she lifted. His
hand caressed her thigh while his other hand tweaked her
nipple.

"Now, Sarah. I need to be inside you now." He
thrust in her hand.

She positioned his tip at her entrance and lowered
herself as he pushed upward. He nipped her ear and she
gasped as he filled her.

"You feel so good. You always feel so good." His
words were thick and hot with desire, making her ride him
faster.

He kissed her neck as his hand moved from her
thigh to her clit, stroking and teasing as he thrust into her.
She rocked against him. The feel of him inside her and
rubbing against her spinning her out of control. Her
movements became frantic, frenzied as she reached her
peak. Her hips bucked as she came and she clenched down
around him. He groaned against her neck as he found his
release. She relaxed against him, resting her face against
his heart. His arms wrapped around her, holding her tight.
She wanted to remember this moment, the feel of him
surrounding her, because soon memories would be all she
had.

See below for a sneak peek at The Voyeur

(Patrick's story). And it's free on all ebook

retailers.

If you're not already a member, join my

Readers' Group.

Here's What You Get When You

Join My Readers' Group

Win Before You Can Buy
Exclusive Giveaways
Free Books
Sneak Peeks

Email me for details:

authorellisoday@gmail.com

The Voyeur

CHAPTER 1: ANNIE

Annie finished making the bed and gathered the sheets from the floor, keeping them as far away from her body as possible. These sex rooms were disgusting and Ethan was a jerk making her work as a maid. She almost had her Bachelor's Degree in Culinary Arts, but he'd refused to hire her for the kitchen—too many men in the kitchen. The only job he'd give her at La Petite Mort Club was as a maid and unfortunately, she needed the money too badly to refuse.

She stuffed the dirty sheets into the cart and hurried out the door. She had almost thirty minutes before she had to be at the next "sex room." She hid the cart in a closet and darted down a back hallway, staying clear of the cameras. Julie, the woman who supervised the daytime maids, was a real bitch. If she were caught sneaking away from her duties, she'd be assigned to the orgy rooms every day. Right now, they all took turns cleaning that nightmare. She swore they should get hazard pay to even go in those rooms.

She slipped through a doorway and hurried to the one-way mirror. She stared at the couple in the next room. From her first day here, she'd been curious about the activities at the club. She was twenty-four and wasn't a virgin but she'd never, ever done some of these things.

The woman in the room below was tied to a table, legs spread and wearing some sort of leather outfit that left her large breasts free and her crotch exposed. She had shaved her pussy and her pink lower lips were swollen and glistening from her excitement. The man strolled around the table as if he had all night. He still had his pants on but had removed his shirt. His arms and chest were well defined but he had a slight paunch. His erection tented his pants and Annie felt wetness pool between her legs. She had no idea why watching this turned her on but it did. Ever since she'd accidentally barged in on that guy and girl in the Interview room, she couldn't stop watching.

The man below ran his hand up the woman's inner thigh, glancing over her pussy. The woman thrust her hips upward and Annie ran her own hand between her legs. The man's mouth moved but Annie couldn't hear anything and then he slapped the woman across the thigh hard enough to leave a red mark. Annie jumped. She wasn't into that, but she couldn't stop watching the woman's face. At first, it'd contorted in pain but then it'd morphed into pleasure. The man hit her again and then bent, kissing the red welts—running his tongue across them as his fingers squeezed her nipple.

Annie clutched her thighs together, searching for some relief. Her panties were soaked. It wouldn't take but a few strokes to make her come. She started to slide her hand into her pants.

"Having fun?" asked a deep voice from behind her.

She spun around, her heart dropping into her stomach. "Ah...I was just finishing cleaning in here." Damn, she should've closed the door but she hadn't expected anyone in this area. The rooms were off limits on this floor until tonight and she was the only one assigned to clean here.

He shut the door and locked it before strolling toward her. She'd seen him around the Club, but more than that she remembered him from the military photos her brother, Vic, had sent to her. She carried one of the three of them—Vic, Ethan and this guy, Patrick—in her purse. He'd been attractive in the picture, but now that he was older and in person he was gorgeous. He had dark green eyes, brown hair and a perfect body. He stopped so close to her his chest almost brushed against her breasts. She was pretty sure it would if she inhaled deeply. She really wanted to take that deep breath and feel his hard chest against her breasts.

"Don't let me stop you from enjoying the show."

"I...I wasn't. I should go." She started to walk past him but he grabbed her hand.

His grip was warm and strong but loose enough that she could pull free if she wanted. She didn't. Even though she only knew him from her brother's pictures and letters, she'd had many fantasies about him when she'd been in high school. Her gaze dropped to the front of his pants and her mouth almost watered. He was definitely interested. She dragged her eyes up his body, stopping on his face. He smiled at her.

"There's nothing to be embarrassed about. Watching turns us all on." He kissed the back of her hand and she jumped as his tongue darted out, tasting her skin.

"I...I should go." She didn't move.

"No, you should watch." He dropped her hand and grabbed her shoulders, gently turning her toward the mirror. He trailed his hands up and down her arms. "Watch."

The man in the other room was now sucking on the woman's breast as his fingers caressed her pussy.

"Would you like to hear them? Or do you like it quiet?" His voice was a rough whisper against her ear.

"Sound, please." She wanted to hear their gasps and moans. She wanted to close her eyes and pretend it was her. She shifted, squeezing her thighs together.

He chuckled as he moved away. She felt his absence to her bones. He'd been strong and warm behind her and for a moment she'd felt safe, safer than she had since her brother had come back from the war, broken and sad, and her father had started drinking again.

The woman's moans filled the room and Patrick came back to stand behind her, this time placing his hands on her waist.

"I'm Patrick," he said against her ear.

She couldn't take her eyes from the scene in front of her. The woman was almost coming as the man thrust his fingers inside of her.

"What's your name?" He nipped her neck and she jumped.

"I...I..." If she told him her name, he might say something to Ethan. Ethan would kill her if he knew she was in here watching.

"Tell me your name." His lips trailed along her neck and she tipped her head giving him better access.

The guy was kissing his way down the woman's body. Annie wanted to touch herself, to make herself come but Patrick was here.

He nibbled her ear. "Why won't you tell me your name?"

"I...I'll get in trouble." She rubbed her ass against his erection, hopefully giving him a hint.

"Tease." His hand drifted down her stomach, stopping right above where she wanted him to touch. "Tell me your name or I'll make you suffer." He unbuttoned her pants and left his hand—warm, rough but immobile—resting on her abdomen.

"I can't." She stood on tip-toe, hoping his hand would lower a little but he was too tall or she was too short. He had to be almost six foot and she was barely five-foot four. "I could get fired and I need this job."

"Darling, Ethan won't fire you for fucking a customer."

"We can't." She spun around. She hadn't thought this through. He was her fantasy come to life and she wanted him to be hers just for a moment, but Ethan would find out and then she'd be in deep shit.

"Don't worry. I'm a member and you work here, so we're both clean." He hesitated, his hands tightening on her hips. "Are you protected?"

"What?" She had no idea what he was talking about.

"Ethan makes sure everyone at the Club is clean but only the…some of his employees are required to be on birth control." He ran his hands up her sides, getting closer and closer to her breasts. "Are you on birth control?" His eyes darkened as they dropped to her tits. "If not, it's okay. There are other things we can do."

Oh, she wanted to do everything his eyes promised, but she couldn't. "No, I'll get in trouble. I need this job. I have to go." She tried to move but her feet refused to obey, so she just stared at his handsome face.

"Are you sure?" He bent so he was almost eye level with her. "I promise. Ethan won't care. A lot of maids become…change jobs. The pay's a lot better." His eyes roamed over her frame. "Especially, for someone as cute as you."

Ethan would kill her before letting her become one of his pleasure associates.

"I could talk to Ethan for you." His hands moved up her body, stopping right below her breasts.

Her nipples hardened and she forgot everything but what he was making her feel. He ran his thumb over one of them and she leaned closer, wanting him to do it again.

He did. He continued rubbing her nipple as he spoke. "I could persuade him to let me…handle your initiation into club life."

Her heart raced in her chest. It could be just her and him doing all these things she'd seen. Her pussy throbbed but she couldn't do it. She wouldn't do it. She couldn't have sex for money. Her parents were both dead but they'd never understand and she couldn't disappoint them. "No. I can't do that…not for money." Her eyes darted to the door. She needed to get out of there before she did something she'd regret.

"That's even better." He smiled as he stepped closer. "We can keep this between us. No money. Only a man and a woman." He leaned down and whispered in her ear, "Giving each other pleasure. A lot of pleasure. In ways you haven't even imagined."

There were moans from the other room and she glanced over her shoulder. The man's face was buried between the woman's thighs.

Patrick turned her around, pulling her against him and wrapping his arms around her waist. "Are you wet?"

"What? No." She struggled in his arms, her ass brushing against his erection again.

"Oh fuck. Do that again." He kissed her neck, open mouthed and hot.

She stopped trying to get away. She wanted this…this moment. She shouldn't but she did, so she wiggled her butt against him again. He was hard and long and her body ached for him. It'd been too long she'd had sex. She needed this.

"Would you like me to touch you?" His hands drifted over her hips and down her thighs.

She'd like him to do all sorts of things to her. She nodded.

"Say it." His words were a command she couldn't disobey.

"Yes."

"Yes, what?" He untucked her shirt from her pants.

"Touch me. Please." She was already pushing her hips toward his hand. She wanted his hand on her, his fingers inside of her.

"Are you wet?" he asked again.

She inhaled sharply as he unzipped her pants.

"Don't lie to me. I'll find out in a minute."

She'd never talked dirty during sex and she wasn't sure she was ready to do that with a stranger. Her heart skipped a beat. Maybe, she shouldn't be doing any of this with a stranger. She grabbed his hand. "Maybe, we shouldn't."

The woman below cried out and the man straightened, wiping his face and unbuttoning his pants.

"Watch. The main event is about to happen." Patrick's hot breath tickled her neck.

Her gaze locked on the man's penis. It was large and demanding. He straddled the woman, grabbing his cock.

"Don't you want to feel some of what they feel?" He nibbled on her ear and then neck. "I can help you."

She may not know him, but she trusted him. He was a former marine. He'd been a good friend of Vic's. He wouldn't hurt her and she needed to come. She loosened her grip, letting go of his hand. He slipped inside her pants, caressing her pussy through her underwear. His fingers were long and strong. She closed her eyes, leaning against him as he stroked her.

"You're already so wet and hot." His breath was a warm caress on her ear. "But, I'm going to make you wetter and then, I'm going to make you come." His other hand shoved her pants down, giving him more room to work. "Open your eyes and watch the show."

She did as he said. The man was inside the woman, thrusting hard and fast. The woman was moaning and trying to move but the restraints kept her mostly helpless.

"Fuck, you're soaked." Patrick's hand cupped her and she arched into his touch, rubbing her ass against his erection. He shoved his hand inside her underwear, his finger running along her folds until he slipped one inside.

"Oh." She grabbed his hand—not to push him away, but to make sure he didn't leave.

He smiled against her hair. "Don't worry, baby. I won't stop." He stroked his finger inside of her and his wrist brushed against her clit.

She needed more. She needed to touch him, feel him. She turned her head, wrapping her arms up and around his neck. He kissed her. It was desperate and wild, but he stopped too soon.

"They're almost done. You don't want to miss it."

She turned back to the mirror. The man below continued to fuck the woman as Patrick finger-fucked her. His other hand slipped under her shirt to her breast. His lips sucked her neck as he rocked his erection against her ass. He was everywhere, and she was so close. The muscles in her legs constricted. Her hips tipped upward.

"Wait, baby," he groaned in her ear, as he pushed a second finger inside of her. "Just a few more minutes."

His fingers were stretching her and it felt wonderful. She moaned, long and low as he thrust harder and faster, almost matching the pace of the man in the other room. She could almost imagine it was Patrick's cock and not his fingers inside of her.

"Oh…oh," she cried out. He was pushing her toward the edge. Her body was spiraling with each pump of his fingers. She was going to come—right here while watching that couple. It was so dirty and so wrong and it only made her hotter.

The woman below screamed and her body stiffened. The man thrust again and again and then grunted his release.

"Show's over." Patrick nipped her neck at the same time he pressed down on her clit with his thumb, sending her shooting into her orgasm.

She trembled and he pulled her close, his hand still cupping her pussy and his fingers still inside of her. When her heartbeat had settled, he removed his hand and bent, pulling off her shoes and removing her pants before lifting her and carrying her to the wall.

"My turn." He wrapped her legs around his waist.

Her phone rang. "My work phone. I...I have to answer it."

"When we're done." He unzipped his pants.

"Annie, answer the phone. I know you're around here. I can hear it ringing you stupid bitch," yelled Julie.

"Oh, shit." She shoved Patrick away, and ran across the room, grabbing her clothes off the floor. "It's my boss. She'll kill me if she finds me like this."

"I'll take care of Julie." He headed for the door, zipping up his fly. "Don't move." He grinned over his shoulder at her. "You can take off your pants again, but other than that, don't move."

"No. Please." She raced over to him, grabbing his arm. "I need this job." And Ethan could not find out about this.

"She won't fire you. She can't. Only Ethan can fire you." He bent and kissed her.

His lips were gentle and coaxing this time and her body swayed into him. He pulled her even closer and she could feel his cock, thick and heavy, pushing against her. Her pussy tightened again in anticipation.

"Damnit, Annie. This is going to be so much worse if I have to call your stupid phone again. Get out here!" Julie was only a few doors down.

She grabbed Patrick and tugged on his hand. "Please, hide." She glanced around, looking for somewhere that would conceal a six-foot muscular man.

"I'm not going to hide from Julie."

Coming soon:

MATTIE'S STORY
ETHAN'S STORY
TERRY'S STORY

Email me with questions, concerns or to let me know what you thought of the book. I love hearing from readers.
authorellisoday@gmail.com

Follow me.

Facebook
https://www.facebook.com/EllisODayRomanceAuthor/

Twitter
https://twitter.com/ellis_o_day

Pinterest
www.pinterest.com\AuthorEllisODay

ABOUT THE AUTHOR

Ellis O. Day loves reading and writing about love and sex. She believes that although the two don't have to go together, it's best when they do (both in life and in fantasy).

Made in the USA
Middletown, DE
11 November 2022

14753180R00126